"Trust me," Sloan

"Give me one reason why I should trust you,"
Jesse said sharply, knowing she was
overreacting because of her uncomfortable
physical awareness of him. All she could
focus on was Sloan's hand resting on hers.

There was a long pause. He didn't move
away, but his fingers suddenly were cold. She
felt the warmth drain out of him like blood,
leaving his face the color of ashes.

"I told Michael I would take care of you," he
said, softly.

Jesse hated seeing him like this. It bothered
her that she had such a strong reaction to
him. Sloan was a very complicated man—
surly and judgmental one moment, charming
and lighthearted the next. And there was such
pain in his eyes.

Suddenly she felt the overwhelming urge to
hold him, comfort him. It didn't make
sense—she hardly knew him. But she wasn't
going to fight her instincts.

Tracy Morgan begins her days with a cup of coffee and an hour spent watching TV news shows before getting her two sons off to school and herself off to work. One morning a story caught her interest—how families of hostages cope. Another cup of coffee. What if, she thought, a young woman's husband was taken captive and he died? By her third cup, *Michael's Wife* became a story begging to be written. But there was a day job to handle and kids to cook supper for. Fortunately, all that coffee made it difficult to sleep nights, so Tracy's first Temptation novel was written.

MICHAEL'S WIFE

TRACY MORGAN

TORONTO • NEW YORK • LONDON
AMSTERDAM • PARIS • SYDNEY • HAMBURG
STOCKHOLM • ATHENS • TOKYO • MILAN
MADRID • WARSAW • BUDAPEST • AUCKLAND

Published February 1993

ISBN 0-373-25530-6

MICHAEL'S WIFE

Prologue

"SLOAN, WAKE UP."

The voice was a whisper in the silence of the night.

"Go away. I'm sleeping."

"Please, Sloan. I need you."

"Shut up!" He shut his eyes tight. "I don't see you. I don't want to see you. You aren't real."

"I *am* real, Sloan," the figure in the moonlight said insistently. "You can shut your eyes or put your pillow over your head like last night, but I'm still here. Feel me."

And then, he could feel her. His skin caught fire at her first, tentative touch, responding to the feather-light pressure of her hand sliding over his bare chest. He gritted his teeth as she touched his leg, then groaned as her fingers brushed against his crotch before moving higher to curl around his erection. He hated himself for surging against her hand, yet he wasn't able to stop his hips from thrusting upward.

"Come to me, Sloan," she crooned, stroking him harder, more rapidly. "Let me lie down beneath you so we can really be together. Love me, Sloan. I want you to—"

"No!"

J. Sloan Lassiter jerked upright in bed, throwing back the sheet and blanket in a violent motion. "Get out of my head, lady. You're driving me crazy!"

He swung his feet to the side of the plain narrow bed and winced as they came in contact with the coldness of the bare floor tiles. He sat for a moment, feeling the slick of sweat from the dream chilling his skin. His body ached—all of it, not just his unsatisfied erection.

Not a sound broke the stillness. He imagined he could hear the echo of his own voice sinking into the thick walls of the room.

"Room, hell!" he muttered.

It was a cell, pure and simple. He looked around in the darkness. A faint shaft of moonlight coming through the grillwork over the window enabled him to see his surroundings. Not that there was anything much to look at—a cheap wooden table stacked with books and papers, a couple of rickety chairs, an old metal footlocker at the end of his bed, and the empty bed on the opposite side of the room: Michael's bed.

Sloan stared at the other bed, bare and stripped of even the rough sheets that used to cover the lumpy mattress. It was the worst part of being here, now. Worse than the long months of being held captive, worse than the magazines and newspapers full of gaping holes. Worse than knowing he might never get out of here alive.

Seeing that bed, empty. Knowing Michael was dead.

"Damn you, Michael. I wish I'd never laid eyes on you."

Sloan buried his face in his hands, trying to block out all memory of Michael Varner. If he hadn't met the fresh-faced kid on the flight from Athens to Cairo, things would have turned out differently for both of them. But it had just been such a kick to see the gleam of excitement in Michael's eyes as they'd neared Egypt. God, how long had it been since he'd felt that kind of excitement about anything, much less about traveling or his job?

He had been returning back from a week of meetings with the executive board of Transco Petroleum, and hadn't been looking forward to the inevitable round of haggling over disputed oil leases. Instead of experiencing the old familiar anticipation at the prospect of making deals and solving problems, he felt an unusual sense of discontentment and uneasiness.

Perhaps he was just bored. He remembered a time not that long ago when he'd enjoyed his work. The Middle Eastern culture and people had been so different from that of America and Europe, it had been a novelty and a challenge for a while. But now, he could walk along the streets, past booths of noisy vendors and beggars and women in their dark veils and long dresses, without even being aware of the exoticism that had so piqued his interest in the beginning. Or maybe he was losing his edge.

No, he hadn't always been this way. He used to thrive on dealing with the oil ministers, and Transco had been so pleased with his negotiating successes that they had given him a pretty free hand in setting up his schedule and procedures. Their trust had paid off, too—well enough that his reputation for deal making had been the subject of a two-page spread in *Newsweek* magazine. These days, he was able to work on his own most of the time, which was a welcome relief after all the red tape of Army life.

The real problem was that he was getting too old for all the politicking involved. He also had to admit that the allure of a nomadic desert life was wearing a little thin. He was close to the point of screaming at the sight of sand dunes and palm trees, and if he never ate another stuffed grape leaf or dish of couscous, it would have been no great loss. He'd just about had his fill of spending half his waking hours waiting for audiences with one minor sheik or another so he could talk to the prince of yet another tiny, isolated principality who could actually cut a deal. Then he would have to spend still more time trying to convince the stuffed shirts in accounting back in New York that he'd finagled the best terms possible. The whole process was becoming tedious and routine.

Yeah, *that* was what was getting stale—not him! The realization was a slight consolation and eased his blue mood. He knew the world revolved around oil shipments, but he was fed up with devoting his whole life to the process.

In a few more hours he would be back in Egypt, resting in his room in the hotel he used as a base of operations in the Middle East. It was a four-star, high-class place. For Transco's top field representative, though, money was never an issue. Hell, they paid him so much these days, it was only a way of keeping score. And the staff at the hotel knew him and made him feel as much at home as he felt anywhere.

To tell the truth, he spent so much time traveling, even this airplane was as commonplace to him as most people's backyards. Sloan shifted impatiently in his seat and stared out the tiny window at the endless blue of sky and ocean below.

His seatmate must have interpreted his restless movement as a sign that he was in need of companionship. The young man kept trying to draw him into a conversation—a feat that Sloan acknowledged took guts. He knew he didn't look like the kind of man people found easy to approach. He looked too much like his father, sharing the same stern features and ice-blue eyes that had kept both the colonel's family and the troops he commanded at a safe arm's distance. In the five years since his father's death, Sloan had seen his own face take on more and more of the hardness that William Lassiter had been renowned and feared for. It wasn't exactly a face that conjured warm memories.

Yet the fearsome Lassiter demeanor hadn't deterred Michael Varner at all. Michael had launched into a breezy account of his trip, and before Sloan knew it, he was actually smiling at the younger man's wry, self-deprecating humor. In the time it took for the stewardesses to bring drinks and serve what the airline passed off as lunch, Sloan had learned enough about Michael Varner to write a short biography.

Michael told him about his family, his wife, and the university where he was doing postgraduate work in archaeology. Most of his conversation, though, had focused on this trip. An ancient city off the coast of Israel had been recently uncovered during construction-site excavation. Michael was one of the lucky few Americans chosen to work on the dig. Evidently his wife hadn't been too fond of his leaving for the three-month project, but that seemed to be his only reservation about it. Sloan thought to himself that the boy was far too young and unfocused to be married in the first place, but he kept his mouth shut.

By the time they landed in Cairo, Sloan discovered he liked Michael Varner. The next thing he knew, he'd invited the kid out to dinner that evening. After all, he knew the best restaurants in the city. No sense in a stranger having to take potluck all alone when Sloan had to eat, anyhow.

"Why didn't you mind your own business that day, Lassiter?" he muttered, looking around the grubby walls that enclosed him in his lonely cell. "Why didn't you just tell him to go to hell and leave it at that?"

If he had only gone his own way as usual, none of this would ever have happened—at least, not to anyone but himself. He didn't want to remember the rest, but it played again in his head like a bad dream. Over and over, he remembered.

From the airport they had taken a cab to the restaurant, one of Sloan's favorites in the city. During dinner, Michael talked and Sloan listened, fascinated by the stories of life in the bosom of a storybook family. Before the evening was over, Sloan found he knew more about the Varner clan than he did about his own family—and especially, more about Michael's beautiful wife, Jesse.

From the first glimpse of her in one of the half-dozen photos Michael carried in his wallet, Sloan knew it was a good thing he'd met Michael alone. If Michael had been traveling with his wife, Sloan would have reacted far differently. As much as he hated to admit it, he would probably have taken a long, lustful look and then closed himself off. This was definitely not the kind of woman he messed around with. This kind of woman was big trouble—married or not.

Even in the photographs, a rare kind of sensuality was evident—a slumberous, seductive aura. She had a thick mane of wheat-blond hair and thick-lashed, heavy-lidded brown eyes that promised all kinds of things. Her mouth was full and not quite smiling.

Sloan had swallowed hard and looked back at Michael, trying not to show his shock that this woman was married to the all-American boy. He didn't do a very convincing job of hiding his curiosity and surprise.

"I saw her first, buddy," Michael had said, laughing and not at all offended by Sloan's unasked question. "It pays to grow up right next door. Jesse fell in love with me before she even knew guys like you existed."

"Just my luck."

Although he'd kept his voice even and light, Sloan wasn't totally kidding. All of a sudden, he wished he had never given in to the impulse to talk to this young man. He wasn't a masochist, and sitting and listening to stories about Michael's wife and family was becoming painful. His own experience of family life had made him a devout skeptic. The kind of life Michael described didn't exist outside the world of old black-and-white television series.

Still, he had to admit Michael's life was just the kind of life he had dreamed of during all his years as an Army brat, moving from one military base to another. But he'd found that carrying around those fantasies hadn't made reality easier to live with—just the opposite.

He had looked across the table at Michael and decided it still didn't make him happier to know someone else had all the things he dreamed of. Sloan brought the evening to an abrupt halt, pleading an early appointment the next day. He intended to drop Michael off at his hotel and spend the rest of the evening trying to forget they'd ever met. There was no reason to explain his sudden mood swing—even to himself it sounded petty.

Hey, kid, I'm jealous of your life, of your woman. I don't want to see you right now. It makes it too clear just how screwed up my own life is.

No, it would be better to say a casual "So long, see you later" and forget this kid and his sexy wife, once and for all. It had been a good idea, a sensible method of damage control. It would have worked, too, except for one little hitch—four men in black hoods grabbed them in the darkness beyond the well-lit entrance to the restaurant. Although such things happened to Americans traveling abroad, Sloan had never anticipated a kidnapping attempt in what he considered to be safe territory. The political situation had been calm in Egypt for a long time then—it wasn't as if they were in Lebanon or Iraq. Things like that weren't supposed to happen here.

Judging by the weapons two of them were carrying—lethal state-of-the-art Uzi machine guns—Sloan knew that they were deadly serious and well trained, undoubtedly with military backgrounds, if their rapid, precise attack was any indication. They never spoke a word, neither to their targets nor to each other.

Despite the abductors' weapons, Sloan might have tried to escape in that split second while there was time to make such a move—might even have had a chance of making it—but Michael's presence made a difference. With the years of martial arts he had studied in the army, Sloan might have had a fighting chance—a very slim chance against four armed men. And if he hadn't made it, risking his own life would have inconvenienced Transco, but there was nobody else who would have been hurt. But things were different for Michael. Michael had a family—he had Jesse. Sloan had hesitated for a moment, and after that pause, the opportunity to put up a fight was gone.

Before he could warn Michael not to resist, his mouth had been sealed with a strip of black electrical tape and his hands roughly bound behind his back in the same fashion. He had only a glimpse of a struggling Michael being similarly trussed before a loose-fitting hood was jerked down over his head. Someone half dragged, half led him a dozen steps before he was lifted up and shoved into what must have been the back of a truck.

Sloan shook his head, pushing away the vivid memory, and looked once more around the hateful little room. The damned bed was still there. All his worry about protecting the kid had been as futile as wishing they had never met. All it had done was prolong the inevitable.

Michael would never make it home to Jesse.

1

GOD, HOW SHE MISSED Michael!

Jesse pushed the painful thought away and forced herself to focus all her attention on maintaining a steady, constant rhythm. *Slap, slap.* Her hot-pink Reebok jogging shoes raised a small cloud of red dust with every step.

The hard-packed dirt of the path was like concrete beneath her feet as she turned and started the home lap of her run. She had taken the well-worn hiking trail instead of the easier route by the highway, assuming the earth would provide more protection for her legs than the man-made surface, but as dry as things were this summer, it probably didn't make much difference.

The drought had hurt the whole state, although they had gotten off a lot easier here than in some parts of the country. There was still enough moisture for the cattle to have good grazing, and the streams were running with enough trout to keep the tourists happy. The scenery was somewhat the worse for wear—the grass was gray-brown instead of lushly green. But anyway, it was getting close to autumn, when everyone would forget the dry, hot summer and start praying for an early snowfall. Michael had always said that Taos didn't really come to life until ski season started.

Jesse concentrated on keeping her pace steady despite the slight down slope of the trail. The terry-cloth band around her forehead was decidedly damp, and her

T-shirt and running shorts clung to her body. She had long since passed the stage of ladylike perspiration her mother would have found acceptable for a well-brought-up young woman. She smiled, imagining how her petite, proper mother would react to the sight of her drenched with healthy sweat.

Thank heavens, Mama was safely back home in Dallas with Daddy to look after. Keeping a watchful eye on the good Reverend Green and visiting with needy members of his congregation kept Carolyn Green too busy for much long-distance fussing over her only daughter. Ever since word had come to them that Michael was dead, her mother's overprotectiveness had escalated into a full-fledged case of smother love. Fortunately, being a state away kept both of them from going over the edge.

Still, there were letters and home-baked goodies that arrived every week in the mail and a phone call every Thursday night. Jesse claimed she found her mother's persistent coddling unnecessary. Still, she did make a point of being at home when it was time for the telephone to ring.

Off in the distance, Jesse could see the elementary school where she taught. In only a few more weeks, the empty playground would be teeming with kids. She was eager to meet the new group of first-, second- and third-graders to whom she would teach art. They might be cranky in reading period or give their math teacher fits, but most of them loved art class.

All the kids knew that "Ms. Varner" was an easy touch. Even in her student teaching days, Jesse had been warned that she needed to be a stricter disciplinarian. Michael had laughed at the notion and said that she enjoyed the circus atmosphere of her classroom because it was such a contrast to the quiet orderliness she had grown up in.

He was right about that. No, he *had been* right. She corrected herself mentally, not giving in to the tendency to think of Michael in the present tense anymore. It was still hard not to imagine him being involved in every aspect of her life.

From the time she was seven years old and Michael's family had moved into the old Jarred place right next door to the parsonage, the two of them had been inseparable. He had walked her home from school, sat beside her in church every Sunday, and escorted her to her high-school prom. There was hardly a memory of her childhood and adolescence where Michael wasn't in the picture. Even now, it was difficult to do anything without having the urge to talk to Michael about it. Sometimes she wondered if the loss would ever get any easier to bear.

No more of that, Jesse silently scolded herself. *You can't spend the rest of your life feeling sorry for yourself. Don't think about it.*

She wasn't supposed to be thinking of Michael at all right now—not while she was running. That had been the whole point of the daily workout schedule. The book she was reading recommended a demanding physical routine as an important step in dealing with the death of a loved one.

"Think only of the activity," she told herself, quoting the author. "Focus total attention on yourself, on your body. Learn to get in touch with yourself physically."

It was good advice. Sometimes it even worked. Then there were days like today—days when she had to run until she was exhausted before her mind turned off and

the physical sensations crowded out the bittersweet
memories.

Jesse tried harder, concentrating totally on the
movement of her body. She noticed how tanned her legs
were getting as she lifted her knees deliberately higher.

Her healthy brown skin was a big improvement over
her pallor when she started running early in the spring.
At first her body had been terribly out of shape. It had
taken her twice as long, then, to cover the three miles.

Her arms pumped in counterpoint to her feet and she
was aware of the pulsing of blood in her veins, of her
slightly labored breathing. It was good to be able to feel
again after all those months of being too numb to care
what kind of shape she was in.

She ran on, grateful for her gradual reawakening to
life. Her hair swished against her neck—a damp, thick
ponytail that bounced between her shoulder blades.
Sometimes she felt a little guilty about her hair. It was
too long, altogether too wild for a widowed, twenty-
seven-year-old schoolteacher.

Most of the time she kept it braided or coiled neatly
at her neck, but she didn't have the heart to cut it. Michael had always loved her hair—had loved to twine
his long, fine-boned fingers in her mass of curls and pull
her close enough to bury his face in it.

"What a pair we make, Jesse," he would murmur. "I'll
bet we're going to have the prettiest, blondest little
babies in the world one of these days. Especially if they
take after their daddy." Jesse would playfully pretend
to push him away, but he would hold her and they
would giggle and kiss. After a while the teasing would
stop and the kisses would deepen. Then he would love
her sweetly and whisper, "Let's make a baby together,
Jesse."

But they had waited to finish college, then for him to get through graduate school, thinking they had all the time in the world.

There had never been any babies. And now there never would be.

Don't think, she ordered herself. *Just run.*

The speed of her motion stirred a slight breeze around her damp skin as she ran, cooling the sweat enough to raise delicious prickles of gooseflesh for a brief moment. Her nipples tightened voluntarily, hardening with an intensity that was simultaneously uncomfortable and strangely pleasant. Jesse glanced down at her gently bobbing breasts watching as the pointed tips became visible even through the double thickness of her bra and T-shirt.

It was a good thing she ran alone these days. She wouldn't be able to hide her now frequent episodes of physical arousal from even the most casual observer. Since she had never considered herself to be particularly hot-blooded, it had been a little embarrassing at first, coming to terms with this blatant sexual awareness. Her lovemaking with Michael had always been good, but sex had never been something she had given all that much thought to. Lately, though, her body had reminded her that she was more of a woman than she had ever realized.

Getting turned on running, of all things! The first time she had recognized the sensation for what it was, she was a little ashamed of herself for having such strong erotic feelings under what certainly couldn't be considered normal circumstances. Whatever the cause—whether she was entering her sexual prime or she'd been alone too long—she was learning to accept it.

If she was going to be honest with herself, she was coming to look forward to the sexual rush that overtook her near the end of each day's run, and to enjoy it. It was private and harmless, and God knew it was a lot less risky than chasing after the men who hung out at the local bar. Her friend Bobbie was being none too subtle in her hints that it was time for her to start dating. So far, Jesse hadn't met a single man who made her forget Michael long enough to get beyond a phone call. It was easier to turn her energies into a long hard run than to play meaningless games with men who left her feeling cold and more alone than ever.

So she ran. Mile after mile. Day after day. Pushing away thought and worry. Trying to keep her mind clear and letting her body have its way.

And these days she didn't try to repress the response of her body to the friction of the cloth against her breasts. Instead, she gloried in the signs of life and desire she had long feared were dead. As she enjoyed the fullness of her breasts, she became conscious of other sensations—heat low in her abdomen and the wet slickness of her lean thighs as they slid back and forth with each step.

The sudden tightness in her muscles had nothing to do with the miles she had covered. She slowed her pace to a fast walk and shook her arms at her sides as she approached the driveway leading up to her house. It was important to cool down gradually, to let her heartbeat return to normal before she went inside. At the front of the house, she put one foot against the porch railing and stretched slowly, feeling the long muscle at the back of her thigh stretch and elongate. She repeated the movement with the other leg.

Her blood was still pounding in her ears when she went inside. The house was quiet and dark after the bright sunlight. She went upstairs to the bedroom.

This was her favorite room in the little house, her private sanctuary. She turned on the stereo and popped in a tape—jazz, with lots of smoky saxophone and a mournful piano. A flick of a switch and the music snaked its way through the intercom until it penetrated into every corner of the house.

She stripped off her clothes and dropped them into the hamper and walked naked to the closet. Her toes curled into the deep, peach-toned carpet, making every step a sensual delight. The white robe she pulled off the hanger was satin, and it felt as luxurious as it looked. She carried it into the bathroom and hung it on a hook on the back of the door, smiling to herself at the small vanity of a woman all alone wearing a dressing gown meant to be appreciated by a lover.

With smooth, economical movements, she drew the shower curtain around the tub and reached inside to turn on the taps, letting the water hiss and fill the room with billowing clouds of steam.

She walked back to the sink, picked up a bottle and poured a generous dollop of its creamy contents into her palm. Slowly, she rubbed her hands together, savoring the musky fragrance. Then she lifted her right leg and propped it on the edge of the sink, flexing and stretching like a dancer at the barre. Beginning at her toes, she lathered her foot with the liquid soap and worked her way up the length of her leg, kneading the swell of her calf, massaging the aching tautness of her thigh. Without haste, she repeated the procedure on her left side.

Next, she poured the shower soap directly onto her shoulders, watching the creamy liquid as it drizzled down over her breasts. She gasped as she touched the puckered buds of her nipples. Sinking her teeth into her lower lip, she felt tension and expectancy beginning to build.

As she lifted her hands and stroked her breasts, she experienced a fleeting sense of unease at giving herself this kind of pleasure, but quickly banished the thought. It was always this way at the start, always not quite what she wanted. But after three lonely years, she knew how to make it good.

She closed her eyes, remembering the way Michael had touched her, and imagined him standing beside her, stroking her.

The two of them had spent many long hours playing in the shower—laughing and splashing, sometimes, or wet and tangled together in a burst of sudden passion. Michael had loved to bathe her, lathering her from head to toe, massaging her soapy skin until she tingled all over. Her body had responded to his touch then, and now—now she wanted to remember it all again.

Michael.

The once-familiar image of his face had eluded her lately, even when she closed her eyes completely and willed herself to think of him. Michael with the laughing blue eyes. Michael, whose golden hair would curl at the slightest hint of dampness.

"Michael," she whispered, trying to evoke the memory of him with her love. "Please, darling. Just one more time."

It was no use. He had gone. No amount of wishing could conjure his face into her fantasies anymore. Jesse choked back a sob of equal parts frustration and sadness. He was gone forever.

She stepped into the far end of the tub, just out of reach of the stinging jets of water. She scrubbed vigorously at her skin with the washcloth, attempting to ignore the persistent craving of her body for fulfillment.

There was a way to give her body and her mind the fix of pleasure it demanded, but Jesse fought against it. As long as she had been able to imagine Michael's presence, it hadn't been so bad, but now...

Now. The heated spray of the water lashed her sensitized skin with an insistent beat. *Now, please.*

For the past month, there had been an image that broke the loneliness, a fantasy that always aroused her and brought her to climax every time. Every time she allowed it, that was. Usually she pushed it away, but it was becoming more and more difficult to resist it. To resist him.

Him. The dark stranger. The dream lover who came to her and, in the heat of passion, made her forget her precious memories of Michael. She had felt dirty at first, and unfaithful, sick about herself for giving in to the mystery lover with such abandon. But, each time it became easier. Each time it became more exciting.

She knew she was going to give in this time. She always did, now. And he never disappointed her, never failed to appear.

She put down the washcloth and reached for the hand-held shower attachment. The fine sharp needles of hot water pulsed over her skin, leaving a tingling trail in their path. Jesse guided the stream of water over her body, playing over her breasts and stomach before she allowed it to linger between her thighs. She shuddered and closed her eyes in surrender, waiting for him to come to her.

And then, he was there. Behind her.

She felt him, barely touching her at first—just the faintest brush of his hair-roughened chest on her back— then his thickly-muscled body molded against the length of her spine, wet and hard and unmistakably male.

He wasn't too tall—almost exactly her height—and when she let her head drop back to rest against his shoulder, he buried his face in her hair. He kissed the tip of her ear, whispering encouragement and making urgent sounds of desire, yet he spoke no words she could understand. Certainly never a word of love.

He gave her what she needed, though—almost all that she needed. He took the water massager from her hands and guided it over her body, lingering for exactly the right length of time on each sensitive spot, arousing her to a fever pitch, then moving on while she was still aching for more.

Her breasts tingled under the stimulating spray. She wriggled and pushed back against him, rotating her hips into his groin. He responded by pressing his hard length between her legs, stroking against her slick heat, yet not entering her, despite her whimpering pleas for him to do so.

With slow deliberation, he parted her legs with his fingers and directed the bursts of warm water between her thighs, supporting her weight as she tensed and ground herself against him in ever more demanding circles. She could feel her orgasm building, threatening to overpower her, to carry her away with awesome force.

All she could think of then was having him inside her, of turning to see his shadowed eyes as she flung herself into the frenzy. He never allowed it to happen. He held her fast and growled passionate sounds of encouragement in her ear and touched her with his hands and with the water until she could hold back the floodtide no longer.

Her body shook with the power of her climax and she arched her back into the pulsating jets of water until the pleasure became too much to bear. She slid down to sit in the tub until her legs regained the strength to hold her upright again.

She couldn't suppress her sharp cry of ecstasy. But her fantasy lover had no face, no name—and Jesse was afraid to open her eyes, knowing he would disappear in a flash of light, as he always had before.

Still, she forced her eyes open, and . . . he was gone. All she saw was the shiny white tile of the tub enclosure, beaded with moisture.

Why did she do this to herself? She didn't feel guilty anymore over the simple act of touching herself, but why did she always have to think of the same man? Always *him?* Although she had never really seen his face, she felt she would recognize him immediately, that she could pick him out of a crowd. It was ironic. She could recognize a stranger, yet she could hardly remember Michael's face. When had she lost Michael and replaced him with this dark and dangerous fantasy lover?

The water continued to pelt down on her, but it was cooler now, far cooler than the hot tears sliding down her cheeks. Jesse sat in the tub and cried, no longer knowing which of her lost lovers she was mourning.

2

THE SLEEK SILVER Maserati sports coupe moved like a shadow over the lonely highway, racing at a furious clip. Inside, J. Sloan Lassiter held the wheel lightly, with only the tips of his fingers controlling the expensive machine. He breathed in appreciatively, reveling as the smell of leather and polish filled his nostrils. Nothing on earth smelled quite like a new car.

There had been long days and endless nights when he had maintained his grip on sanity by thinking about how a new car would smell. Or how an ice-cold beer would taste. Or remembering the sound of a crowd roaring in anger or triumph at a football game.

"Best football team?" Sloan could almost hear Michael's teasing voice even after all this time, young and eager, trying to fill the hours with something to keep their minds occupied during the endless, dreary days. "Quick now, and don't start reliving the glory days of the Dallas Cowboys. Let's say, best football team in *this* decade."

Sloan recalled the long months when he and Michael had played the game. The Best of the Best, they had called it. Best Beatles song. Best pitcher in the Major League. Best pickup line. The game had been a great starting place for conversation, often turning into long, serious discussions.

Sometimes they had argued, usually over politics. There were times when the generation gap was so profound they might have been two generations apart instead of a little more than a decade. Sloan's straight-arrow military background and Michael's student laissez-faire attitude were as opposite as everything else about the two men.

But their differences were what had made the game so successful. Sometimes they had laughed until they couldn't breathe. On a few occasions, their discussions veered into sentimental territory, and they damn near lost their minds. Still, they had gotten by on memories of the past and dreams of the future. Sometimes they barely kept each other from giving up entirely.

One night after about eight months in captivity, Michael had been caught up in a rare bout of depression—a despair so deep that he seemed to be losing his unshakable belief that they would be rescued any day.

"I don't think I can stand it here much longer." Michael stood at the foot of Sloan's bed, shifting his weight back and forth from one bare foot to the other. "I'm not kidding, Sloan. If we don't get out of here, I really think I'm going to lose it."

"Take it easy, kid." Sloan was tired himself and not much in the mood to calm an attack of hysteria. "Just lie down and try to get some sleep."

"Sleep?" Michael's voice made an insult of the word. "I've slept so much, I'm caught up for the next ten years. I don't ever want to close my eyes again."

Michael had been pacing restlessly all evening, back and forth in the small space between their beds. Sloan had been about ready to scream. He had entertained the notion of tying him up or punching him out just to keep him still. Only the frightened wildness in the kid's eyes had given him the patience to grit his teeth and bear it.

There were too many times he had felt exactly the same way, as though the walls were closing in on him. Sometimes moving around helped give the illusion of not being trapped.

"We aren't ever going to get out of here, are we?"

"Come on, Michael. Aren't you the one who plans a new 'great escape' every other week? Let's hear what you have in mind now, and don't give me any more variations on the theme of us digging a tunnel out of here."

"Don't worry. I've given up on the great escape. That kind of stuff only happens in the movies," Michael said bitterly. "We might as well get used to the idea that we're never going to get out of here."

"Never's a long time." Sloan hoped he sounded more cheerful than he felt. He didn't have any idea how they were going to get free, but there was no way he was going to plan on spending the rest of his life in this crummy room. "Something will turn up. Some way. You can't give up now, not when—"

"Not when what? Has something happened to give us any hope? Has something—anything—happened at all since we've been in here that might make today any different from yesterday?" Michael's voice rose, growing shrill with anger and frustration. "God help me, if you can tell me one thing that gives you any hope, I'd sure like to know what it is."

"We're still alive, kid. Still kicking."

"Yeah, and ain't life grand?" Michael threw himself down on the cot, worn out by the futility of anger. "We're not going to get out of here. Ever." He turned his back to Sloan and said in a dull voice, "I'm never going to see my wife again, am I?"

"Sure, you are."

"What if she gets tired of waiting for me? She's so pretty and so wonderful, there are probably a dozen guys trying to make her forget all about me."

"Don't get paranoid and start dreaming up all this stuff to make yourself even more miserable." Sloan was losing his patience. "If half of what you've told me about Jesse is true, she'll be right there waiting for you when you get back, even if it's ten years from now."

"Ten years! God, if I have to stay in this place for ten more days I'll lose my mind. And my wife," he added more quietly. "No woman—not even Jesse—can be expected to live like a nun for that long."

"Give her a little credit. She's got her parents and yours to take care of her."

"There are a few things our folks can't do for her, if you know what I mean." Michael wasn't one to share graphic details about his marriage, but it was obvious what he was worrying about. "For a woman so beautiful, Jesse really hasn't had all that much experience with guys. I mean . . . Well, you know . . . after not having anyone around to . . . be with, what if some other guy comes along? Some smooth talker's probably just waiting around to catch her in a weak, lonely moment and—"

"Don't let your imagination run away with you. Jesse loves you just as much as you love her. She's not going to give up on you. I don't think you have to worry about her running around with anyone else." Sloan thought for a minute before adding, "Besides, she's a preacher's daughter, isn't she? She promised to love and honor and all that stuff for better and for worse. I'll bet she takes that pretty seriously."

"I doubt if she ever thought about things being *worse* for this long." Michael was wallowing in his misery, not giving an ounce of effort to being cheered up. "Would you be willing to wait if you'd gone without for this long?"

"For sex?" Sloan considered the question seriously. His answer surprised even him. "You know, if I had a woman, a wife, that I really loved, I believe I would. I've never met anyone I felt that much of an attachment to. Maybe I'm not ever going to. But, I sure believe it would be important to me to wait."

"And I'm supposed to believe that charming little fairy tale and stop worrying? I remember all the stories about you and your lady friends tearing around Paris and Istanbul," Michael replied skeptically. "Sure, you'd wait. What kind of simple-minded idiot do you take me for?"

"A depressed, self-pitying, simple-minded idiot," Sloan snapped, growing tired of Michael's incessant tirade. "Now stop being so damned pessimistic or just shut up. Even if you don't want to get some sleep, I'm about ready to give up for the night."

"Well, pardon the hell out of me for boring you with my problems. You just go on to sleep. I know you have a busy day penciled in for tomorrow."

Sloan let the slam go without an answer. He was sorry to have hurt the kid's feelings, but it was a relief to hear a touch of anger edging out the pervasive self-pity. When Michael was down, it made his own nightmares about never getting out all the more real.

"BUT YOU DID GET OUT, Lassiter. That's what you have to live with."

Sloan pulled himself back to the present. He looked around as if seeing the flatland stretching out for miles around him for the first time. He pushed down on the accelerator until the countryside disappeared into a dusky blur. The Maserati responded without a second's hesitation.

"You were right, Michael, my friend," he whispered under his breath. "This is the best car in the world."

Best sports car. Now, that had been an ongoing topic of conversation.

"Yeah, that was going to be . . ." Michael had paused for a few seconds, then continued deliberately, "*Is* going to be my reward for finishing school. As soon as I pick up that master's degree, I'm going to go out and buy myself a sports car. Not just any old car, though."

"What kind is it today, Michael?" Sloan liked to bait the kid a little. "Are you still lusting after the cherry-red Porsche coupe? Naw, that was last week's baby. I remember now—the powder-blue Ferrari convertible, right?"

"I'm still thinking about that one. Jesse always thought I should get one to match my eyes. That was about all she knew about cars—things like what color they were or if they had a stick shift. She hates stick shifts." Michael made a sound that started out as a laugh, then broke down somewhere in the middle and ended in a sigh. "Can you believe anyone wanting a sports car with an automatic transmission?"

Michael had sworn he was going to drive his current choice—a Maserati—off the lot, so he could have one no one else had ever driven.

Even near the end, when Michael was getting weaker and sicker every day, he still talked about getting that new car. And he talked about Jesse.

"I wish you could meet Jesse," Michael said between the bouts of coughing that left him weak and his breathing raspy. "You'd love her."

More and more, Sloan's mind played the nasty little trick of supplying visual images of the woman his cell mate described in such vivid and loving detail—especially when he closed his eyes and tried to sleep. Too often he woke up aroused and ashamed, hating himself for betraying his friend, and hating Jesse, too, although he knew she had no guilt in the matter.

It galled Sloan to admit that even at times like now, he had to clamp down hard to keep his subconscious from dwelling on Jesse Varner. Michael was sick, dying probably. How much sicker was it that he was tempted by covetous fantasies under such circumstances?

"Everyone loves my Jesse." Michael could talk of nothing else, it seemed, even when he could barely gasp the words. "She's so beautiful, so . . ."

He trailed off and Sloan thought he was sleeping. There was an irregularity in his breathing now that frightened Sloan. The time between one exhalation and the next labored intake of air seemed to last forever. Sloan found himself silently counting the seconds between the rattles of air.

Six, seven . . .

The air hissed in. Sloan kept vigil, tensed on the bed like a coiled spring.

Six, seven, eight . . .

Again, the breath caught and held, escaping faintly. *Eight, nine, ten . . .*

Sloan held his own breath for a heartbeat.

Eleven. He sat up. *Twelve.* Fear rose sharply in him, raising gooseflesh hackles on his arms. *Thirteen.*

"Mike?"

Fourteen, he heard inside his head.

"Michael, are you okay?"

Fifteen.

He leaped to his feet and reached down to shake Michael, yank him to a sitting position.

"Sloan?" Michael breathed again, but it was a gasping cry for help. "God, Sloan, I can't breathe. I'm so scared."

Michael slumped backward, too weak to remain upright on his own. If not for the iron strength of Sloan's hands grasping him and supporting him, he would have hit the hard mattress.

"It's okay, kid. I'm right here." Sloan felt like cursing at the futility of his presence. There was nothing he could do. Without a doctor or divine intervention, Michael wasn't going to make it through this night. "Just hang on, Michael. It will be morning soon."

"Doesn't matter." It was a faint, apathetic whisper, a pale shadow of Michael's usual vibrant spirit. "I'm too tired.... Too tired to wait for morning anymore. It doesn't matter."

"Like hell, it doesn't matter!" Fear roughened Sloan's voice to an angry-sounding growl. "It matters to me. You hang on. Hear me? You just hang on."

"Wish I could, buddy. Too tired."

Michael sounded sad, but his sorrow had a distant and detached ring to it. Sloan could feel his only real friend in the world slipping deeper into the darkness, his voice fading and his chest barely rising and falling. All he could think to do was to pull the old blanket up around the boy and hold on to him. No one had ever gotten as close to him as this and it hurt more than he knew how to deal with. Michael was dying, and there wasn't a damn thing he could do except sit here and wait for it to be over.

"Sloan?"

"I'm here, Michael. Right here." He tightened his arms around the thin shoulders and wished he believed in miracles. "Can I get you anything? A drink of water?"

"No water." Michael began to shiver slightly.

"Are you cold? Let me get the blanket from my bed—"

"Don't leave." Michael reached up and grabbed his hand, holding it with as strong a grip as his failing body could manage. "Promise me..." He barely got the words past his chattering teeth. "Promise me you'll get out of here."

"We're both going to get out of here, kid." Sloan wanted it to be true so much it was hardly a lie.

"Promise you'll go to Jesse. Tell her..." He closed his eyes and fought for strength to go on. "Tell her I loved her every day...."

"Come on, Michael. Fight it. Fight harder." Sloan was begging in earnest. "Jesse needs you."

"Take care of her for me, Sloan."

Those were the last words Michael ever spoke. He didn't suffer anymore, just closed his eyes and rested against the supporting strength of Sloan's arms. Sloan held him and talked as he'd never talked in his whole life. His words filled the darkness, drowning out the tortured rasping breathing, growing louder as the sinister rattle of death echoed in his head. He wished for the release of tears or the sting of anger at their captors, but anguish kept him dry-eyed.

As the darkness deepened around them and Michael's life ebbed away, Sloan talked about anything he could think of. Even after it was too late, he clung to Michael's body, trying to keep it warm with his own body heat, praying an awkward final prayer because he knew it was important to Michael. He prayed, although he didn't have much faith in God right now. How could God let this happen? Michael should be back in Texas, loving his wife and riding around in the sports car of his dreams. He didn't know if God took any interest in his half-angry prayer, but he vowed to the Almighty that if he ever got out of this dry little piece of hell, he'd do his best to carry out Michael's last wishes.

It was another seventeen months before he was freed from his captors. After all that time and all the great plans for escape, getting free had been totally out of his control. As suddenly and with as little reason as he and Michael were taken, Sloan was released.

In the middle of a dark night, two guards he had never seen before had entered and calmly tied his hands behind his back. Sloan hadn't bothered to struggle against them. After the months of being alone in the tiny room, anything, including death itself, was preferable to this living hell.

They stood him up with his back to a hard wall and faced him, guns drawn. Sloan stared back at them, willing them without words to do it, to just get it over with. Instead, they held a newspaper covered with Arabic headlines in front of him and brought out an old Polaroid camera, snapping three or four flashes in his eyes.

Before the dark spots completely cleared from his vision, one of the men took a hypodermic needle from his jacket pocket and walked to Sloan's side. The last thing he remembered was the sharp bite of the needle in his upper arm and the rough feel of the wall against the skin of his back as he slid down it toward welcome oblivion.

He woke up in a hospital bed in the American embassy in Cairo with no idea how he got there. It was frustrating to lose three years—not knowing where he'd been held or by whom or why. The guys in the gray suits swarmed all over him and brought him back to the States. For weeks they questioned and counseled and questioned again until he began to feel like a prisoner of his own country. Finally, they either ran out of red tape or realized they had no recourse but to release him.

The first thing he'd done then was to go out and buy this car. He'd swallowed hard when he looked at the sticker price, but since he'd collected three years of back pay plus interest, it had hardly made a dent in his bank account. It wasn't as if he had anyone to spend his money on, anyway.

Besides, he felt good thinking about how happy the car would have made Michael. He would have been so pleased to sit behind the wheel, to feel the power of the engine and to know that no one else had put a mile on it. As Michael would have wanted, Sloan had driven the car right off the lot and onto the street. And now he was only a couple of hours away from driving it right up to Jesse Varner's front door.

"You're six kinds of stupid, Lassiter," he growled, glancing at himself in the rearview mirror. "Don Quixote wouldn't have been a big enough idiot to take this on. I'd be willing to bet that Ms. Varner isn't going to appreciate having you turn up uninvited, stirring up old memories. She's probably shut the book on this chapter of her life by now."

He turned his attention back to the road, looking for something to break the sameness of the landscape. He certainly didn't have to concentrate much on his driving—the highway through this part of the country from Dallas to New Mexico didn't exactly offer a scenic view. Except for the mountains he could now see faintly in the distance, the land was so flat and empty that he could have driven across it with his eyes shut. All he'd had to do was slow down for speed traps in some of the smaller towns.

Sloan had spent a lot of time in Texas and New Mexico years before while he was learning about the oil business. After he left the Army, he'd taken a job as an oilfield roustabout, insisting to the CEO at Transco that he was going to train for his job from the bottom up. It had taken more than a year before he was content to move into the overseas position of negotiating leases and supervising contracts—a sweaty, backbreaking year of throwing an oil-slick chain in hundred-degree Texas days and mixing drilling mud in below-zero nights when the wind blew so hard it cut through insulated coveralls like an icy knife.

His father had scornfully written his son off as a failure, not understanding for a minute why he chose to make his mark anywhere besides the service. No amount of talking could convince him that Sloan was little better than a deserter or that his job was ever going to amount to anything. The colonel had no use for civilian life, and on the rare occasions when they had seen each other, Sloan had given up on talking about his new career. In fact, he remembered bitterly, he spent most of his time avoiding doing any talking himself. It only gave his father a chance to lay into him about the rest of his shortcomings—no wife, no children—the list was endless. The last time he saw his father, Sloan had stormed out after the colonel began haranguing him about how Sloan's mother had died without ever having a grandson.

"A grand*son*," Sloan muttered angrily. "I'd probably have screwed that up and had a daughter. God, wouldn't he have made a case of that?"

He smacked the steering wheel with the edge of his hand, making the car swerve toward the center of the road. Sloan reined in his temper and concentrated on driving. The flat, dry land spread out for miles in all directions, farms and ranches with tractors and cattle coexisting with drilling rigs and pumping jacks. But against the endless horizon, the sunsets were spectacular. *Best sunsets—West Texas.* He and Michael had agreed on that one without an argument.

"Damn near all we agreed on," Sloan said, in a half whisper.

The mountains were getting closer now, blue-gray and hazy. Sloan shifted uncomfortably in the deep leather bucket seat. He had driven all day, planning to get into Taos before nightfall so he could make the requisite duty visit and get it over with before morning. But now he found himself considering pulling over for the night at the next halfway-decent motel he came to.

He was too tired to face the hassle and mental effort of another emotional experience tonight. The meeting he'd had with Michael's mother and father had used up all the strength he had, leaving him wrung out and raw. They had seemed genuinely glad to talk with him, accepting and welcoming him as a friend of Michael's and, by extension, a friend of the family. Not once had they made him feel any blame. Not one time had they criticized him for not managing to somehow save Michael. They had even expressed gratitude that he was going to see Jesse. He had felt like a heel over that.

Sitting there in the house he knew so well from Michael's description—right down to the lazy tabby cat curled up on top of the television set—hearing them make him out to be some kind of hero, all he wanted to do was turn tail and run. If only they knew the kind of fantasies he had about Jesse, how different things would be. Instead, he listened to their stories filled with loving memories of their lost son and gave them what pleasant recollections he could, leaving them with the little comfort he had to offer. And when he left their home, he felt more alone than ever.

No, a night's rest before he hit Taos sure as hell couldn't hurt.

"And what makes you think you'll be able to rest while you're in the same state as the luscious Ms. Varner? Not that she's really anything like you've imagined, but it's not her you have to worry about, is it?"

According to Michael's parents, Jesse was nothing at all like the vixen who haunted his dreams. She was teaching school, had settled down in her own home, and solid as the Rock of Gibraltar.

Such a strong girl... handled everything with dignity... never found anyone to take Michael's place....

Their description made him more certain than ever that seeing Jesse Varner was going to be more trouble than it was worth. Just looking her in the eye after recalling all the fantasies he'd indulged in was going to be almost impossible.

"Look, you overaged stud. If you had any brains, you'd gut up and get it over with tonight."

He stared at himself in the mirror again, squinting in the waning light. The face looking back at him was so serious he had to laugh.

"If I had any brains left, I sure as hell wouldn't be holding a conversation with myself. And out loud, for Crissakes."

He laughed, cringing a little as the rusty sound echoed in the plush emptiness of the car. Hell, it was funny, wasn't it—talking to himself and laughing at things that weren't remotely humorous while he drove along the most godforsaken roads in the country in a Maserati he'd never wanted, all because of a promise to a man who'd been dead for nearly two years?

"And people don't think I have a sense of humor? I may be warped, but I swear, this is a funny situation."

He laughed again, but it was forced, even to his own ears. He couldn't let himself stop thinking of this as a rather macabre kind of joke. Not yet. If he made it through the next few hours, he might let down his guard and relax. It would feel good to wipe off the tight smile he'd worn for a month, but he was afraid of what might be hiding underneath.

"And another thing," he reminded himself. "This isn't some Middle Eastern hellhole, you loony bastard. You're back in the real world now, and you've got to learn to follow the rules again, J. Sloan. Normal people don't hold lengthy conversations with themselves. Not on a regular basis."

"So I hear, Mr. Lassiter," he answered in a coarse whisper. "But old habits are hard to break, sir. Maybe I can taper off."

His straight white teeth flashed in a self-conscious grin as he caught sight of himself in the mirror.

"That's what they all say, pal. All those old guys in the home."

He reached up and adjusted the mirror, slanting it so that his face was no longer visible. His neck was beginning to ache and he massaged it absently as he drove. It was getting close enough to dark to switch on the headlights. Once the lights were on, he wondered how he'd been able to see at all without them. The night had come on so gradually that his eyes had adjusted to the encroaching grayness, but the effort had cost him.

Fatigue settled over him as darkness blanketed the countryside. He rolled down the window, letting the hot, dry air replace the air-conditioned coolness. Maybe some music would perk him up a little. He scanned the dashboard, trying to pick out the radio controls from an array of buttons and levers that would have looked right on the Concorde. Once he'd found them, it seemed like a lot of trouble for nothing.

In between noisy bursts of static, he sampled at least two country and western stations, another that featured a Spanish guitarist, and several more that seemed to be playing the same screeching rock band. He listened for a few minutes to a syndicated talk show, then decided that he had too many problems of his own to be interested in hearing about the latest diet craze and how losing forty pounds changed some actress's life.

He had never heard of the woman, but from the callers' gushing comments, he was sure he must be the only person in the country who hadn't. That was the kind of thing that knocked his legs out from under him, that made him angry at having had a big chunk of his life stolen: It was all the small things he had missed—things that everyone knew and never thought twice about knowing.

He punched the Off button on the radio, wishing again that he had taken the time to pick up a few tapes. Something old, maybe the Stones or Bruce Springsteen. Thank God, the Boss was still around and going stronger than ever. It was reassuring to know there were some threads of continuity left to grab hold of.

He hummed and sang his way through his entire repertoire of golden oldies in his gravelly bass, grinning to himself when he forgot the words and filled in with whatever nonsense popped into his head.

Just as he was bored enough to try changing the radio station again, a distant cluster of lights flashed into sight when he rounded a curve in the foothills. It wasn't a large town, but it looked as if it would be big enough to have an all-night café and a couple of motels. Not one to be picky after his accommodations for the past several years, Sloan straightened in the seat and looked for an exit ramp.

HE'D BEEN IN WORSE places. Not often, though, thank goodness. Norman Bates would have found this place rough going. It wasn't chic or run-down or even frightening—it didn't have enough atmosphere to make it interesting. It was just a long line of numbered rooms behind a main office with a flashing Vacancy sign. That was its main selling point—the only Vacancy sign in town.

The desk clerk had given him a thorough once-over, batting her heavily mascaraed lashes and taking an extraordinary length of time to fill out his credit-card receipt. While he signed it, she told him her name was Betty and that he should call her if he needed anything—anything at all.

She was very impressed with his car, and without false modesty, Sloan recognized that she was equally eager in her appraisal of him as a man. He had been out of circulation for a long time, but not long enough to be interested in flirting with her. Despite the heavy makeup and forthright manner, she was just a girl— barely old enough to be up at this hour, much less working the night shift right off the main highway. Even if he had been in need of a woman, this one was as far from the kind he would have picked as chalk was from cheese. His lady friends were cool and sophisticated and unemotional. He'd been told once that he knew how to make love, but he didn't know anything about intimacy. The accusation had been so dead-on, there had been nothing he could say in rebuttal.

Sloan looked at the young receptionist, smiled, and wished her a friendly good-night before he walked out.

Sloan was relieved to find his room wasn't nearly as dreary as the lobby. An hour after he checked in, he felt almost human again. It was amazing what a hot shower and a couple of cold beers could do for a man's disposition. Sloan tied a surprisingly fluffy bath towel around his hips and turned back the bedspread. After fighting off a bad case of drowsiness for a hundred miles, he suddenly found himself wide-awake. Awake and bored.

The quiet, bare room reminded him too much of the solitary cell he had endured for so long. At least, here there was something else to do besides count the cracks in the ceiling, although it wasn't one of his favorite pastimes. He walked to the television set bolted to a metal stand and turned it on.

He didn't bother to try the network channels. He had never developed an addiction to television. Even as a kid he hadn't been allowed to watch very often, but it hadn't been too much of a sacrifice. They had never spent enough time in places where English-speaking programs had been available for him to miss it. He did like movies, though, and these days, thanks to satellite dishes, even isolated places like this were hooked up to several movie channels.

One program caught his attention for several minutes. He watched in idle appreciation as a trio of nubile nymphets strutted around clad only in the bottom halves of their bikinis. Unfortunately, the plot was as skimpy as the costumes, so he flipped the dial. The next choice was a James Bond movie that also had a bevy of beauties, but a somewhat more interesting plot. Sloan didn't recognize the actor playing Bond, but the formula was still the same.

Out of curiosity, he turned the sound down a little and switched off the light, removing his bath towel and automatically folding it into a neat square before he crawled into the bed. He propped a couple of pillows against the headboard and leaned back with a tired sigh.

This wasn't too bad, if you discounted the hour and lack of company. He finished off another beer as he watched the new 007 save the world without ever losing his detached air or his panache. Somewhere between bedding the blonde and the inevitable car-chase scene, Sloan drifted off to sleep. Bond didn't notice.

When he opened his eyes again, Sloan wasn't certain whether he was in the middle of a particularly kinky variation of his usual dreams or if he had finally slipped over the line into insanity. Whichever it was, it was enough to make him break into a fine sweat.

The room was pitch-dark, except for the flickering image on the television screen. Sloan could hear the faint beat of music, hot and pulsating. He could hear his own breathing, ragged with the sudden flash of arousal.

On the screen a woman was dancing, standing in front of a window, taking off her clothes to the music. Her hair was a long, wild tangle of blond that covered her face. Her body was ripe and wicked and restless, twisting and pirouetting as he had seen her do in a hundred dreams.

Jesse.

The woman danced with her back to the camera, preventing him from catching a clear shot of her face. Every time she turned, shadows obscured her features, but he had no doubt it was her. Damn. He had to be losing his mind. That was the only rational explanation. There was no other way to explain how Michael's wife—the woman who had haunted his sleep and intruded into his waking dreams—could suddenly have appeared on the screen in front of him.

Then she tossed her head and stared straight into the camera, and Sloan felt as if his heart had been jerked out of his chest. *It wasn't her.* The woman was blond, sexy and beautiful, but she was nothing at all like Jesse.

Now that he was wide-awake, he saw nothing about the woman to remind him of Jesse other than a superficial resemblance due to her beautiful hair. He let out a long slow whistle of air and struggled to keep from grabbing an empty beer can and hurling it at the flickering screen.

For what seemed to be an eternity, but could only have been a few more minutes, he sat watching the movie, not moving for fear that he couldn't control the surging anger he felt. He didn't get up to adjust the sound, although it was too low for him to make out much of the dialogue. He really wasn't sure why he was so upset. It wasn't because it wasn't Jesse on the screen. This woman was doing things he'd never imagined with Jesse—blindfolding and bondage, food orgies and public lovemaking—things he would never want to see Jesse involved in.

His hands flexed, gripping the sheets on either side of him until his fingers ached. He ached all over, dismissing the tiny woman on the screen, not wanting her despite her sexiness. He only wanted Jesse. He had been able to stand it, just barely, all those other nights, but this was almost more than he could tolerate without screaming. He clenched his fists and watched unblinkingly until the final credits rolled.

"Thank God, it's only a movie," he said aloud. "Jesse Varner is a grade-school teacher, not some movie sexpot."

It was just coincidence that the actress was vaguely of the same physical type as Jesse. And it was only a movie. Yeah, he had known that all along. Hadn't he? That meant he wasn't crazy. Well, not completely crazy.

"Not yet, pal. Let's see what the shrinks say after you meet the real thing."

He closed his eyes again and willed his taut body to relax. He tried hard to banish the images of Jesse Varner and the movie-blonde sex expert. All he needed was one more idea of how he would make love to the woman if he ever got the chance—not that he would really do it.

"Like hell you wouldn't, you low-down dog."

He had to get this out of his mind. All it would take was willpower.

It didn't take him long to figure out that willpower wasn't his strong suit tonight. The bed might as well have been made of cinder blocks for all the rest he got in the next hour. He punched and turned the pillow until it was limp, and ground his teeth so hard, his jaws hurt.

Finally, cursing women in general and sexy blondes in particular, he gave up. He threw back the covers and got up. As he dressed, the next movie started—a slapstick comedy about the adventures of a bunch of incompetent police trainees. He didn't even bother to turn off the television set.

In five minutes he had cleared out his things and loaded his bag into the trunk of the car. It was still hours before sunrise when he pulled back onto the freeway to begin the last leg of his journey to Taos.

3

JESSE WOKE TO the nerve-racking sounds of thunder and jackhammers. She understood where the thunder was coming from—a rainstorm had begun in the hours before dawn. But the intermittent bursts of jackhammering had her wrinkling her forehead in confusion and pain.

Awful pain—her head felt like an overripe melon. She had an overwhelming desire to bury her head beneath the covers, but even in this state, her conscience wouldn't let her go back to sleep without investigating the cause of the infernal racket. It had been great of Gran and Granddad to let her live in the house, but they probably wouldn't appreciate her letting it be torn down while she recuperated from a hangover.

Then, all at once the room was blessedly quiet. Some kind soul had turned the volume down. It must have been the result of divine intervention, because even the driving rain and rumbling thunder receded to a dull roar. Jesse sent up a thankful prayer and a fervent promise to never again drink more than a single glass of wine, no matter what the provocation, and slipped back into dreamland.

The peaceful quiet didn't last long. A loud burst of thunder heralded a downpour of rain so loud it rattled the windowpanes. Jesse groaned and wished she had some cotton for her ears. Then the jackhammer started anew, louder than before. There wasn't enough cotton in New Mexico to block out the cacophony. She reluctantly pushed the blankets back and sat up.

That was her first mistake of the day. Her head throbbed so badly she could feel the blood pulsing in her temples with every heartbeat. She moaned piteously. Her stomach was full of knots. Her legs were as unsteady as a seasick sailor's, and moving her eyes took all the coordination she could muster. Even her hair hurt!

Slowly, Jesse eased her feet onto the floor, grateful for the soft carpet. It would muffle the sound of her footsteps. No one had ever told her that drinking too much intensified the ability to hear. It made her wonder if alcoholics ever developed problems with hearing loss. Suddenly the jackhammer pounding was back with renewed vigor, and she clapped her hands over her ears and winced. Right now, the only hearing problem she cared about was her own.

In a burst of insight, Jesse identified the cause of the noise. It wasn't a jackhammer, after all. It was the front door. Some idiot was banging on her door—some very persistent idiot. She glanced at the clock beside her bed.

"For heaven's sake," she muttered. "It's not even nine o'clock yet. If that's Bobbie, I'll wring her neck. She'd better feel just as rotten as I do."

Jesse didn't bother to pull a robe on over the long T-shirt she wore as nightgown. All she could think of was getting to the door and killing whoever was out there. It had to be Bobbie Stone. After all, she'd left her purse, her cigarette lighter, and several empty wine bottles here last night. Hank hadn't thought it was very funny when he came to pick up his wife only to find the two of them giggling and more than a little drunk.

Oh, he had been very upset with them both last night, if she remembered correctly. And considering how many glasses of wine she and Bobbie had drunk, she wasn't betting on how much she actually did remember.

It had all started off innocently enough. Bobbie had called and asked Jesse if she would like to go to a movie and dinner while Hank and the boys had a Scout-troop cookout at their house. Jesse had taken pity on her friend, having seen the three Stone sons in action. No woman should have to put up with those kids, not to mention the half-dozen other preteen boys who would be there.

When Jesse drove in and picked Bobbie up, the last thing on their minds was getting sloshed. It just sort of turned into that kind of night. The lineup at the theater was so long that they decided to rent a videotape instead. Getting a couple of orders of take-out chicken from the grocery-store deli seemed easier than cooking. And if the wine hadn't been on sale, they wouldn't have ended up with four bottles.

They had eaten and talked while the rented movie played in the background, stopping to watch a scene now and then. But the conversation they shared was more entertaining by far. Bobbie loved to gossip and there was hardly a story in town she didn't know the details of. Jesse had listened, fascinated with the juicy tidbits about the locals, who were almost as interesting as Bobbie herself.

"You're making that up, Bobbie. Admit it."

"I'm doing no such thing. Swear to God." Bobbie's hazel-green eyes twinkled mischievously, even as she crossed her heart and looked toward heaven. "If Junior Duncan hadn't had a couple of old horse blankets in the back of his pickup, those two would have had to ride back to town with him, butt naked."

"Is that why Hank fired him?"

"Lord, no." Bobbie looked up at Jesse from her half-reclining position on the floor. "We may be a small town, and I'll admit Hank can be a real prude sometimes, but that wasn't the reason he let Will go."

"There's something worse than that?" Jesse picked up her glass from the table and finished her wine, frowning when Bobbie sat up and refilled both their glasses. "No more, Bobbie. I don't think my boss would appreciate my getting his wife drunk."

"Shh. School's not in session yet, so don't worry about what the principal thinks," Bobbie shushed, her words beginning to slur. "Besides, he'd never blame you. Everyone thinks you're perfe't. A perfe't teacher, a perfe't little lady."

"That's easy for you to say." Jesse giggled. "Daddy always said it's easy to be perfe't . . . perfect," she corrected, "if you aren't tempted. I haven't had much opportunity to be anything but perfect since Michael went away."

"Bull," Bobbie said sharply. "All you need to do is crook your little finger and you'd have half the single guys in Taos lining up to tempt you. Half the married ones, too, if you were interested."

"Well, I'm not interested. I don't know if I ever will be. There's never going to be anyone who can take Michael's place."

Jesse felt her eyes fill with tears. Her silly mood disappeared and she gave a small hiccup that came dangerously close to turning into a sob.

"Stop that right now, Jesse Varner," Bobbie ordered in a no-nonsense tone. "I've listened to you cry more than enough over the past eighteen months. Enough is enough."

"I'm sorry, Bobbie. But I miss him so much, still."

"Of course you do, Jess. We all do." Bobbie's voice softened, and she reached up to squeeze Jesse's hand in a quick gesture of understanding. "I remember all those winter vacations when the four of us skiied and hung out at your grandparents' place together. I haven't forgotten how you two were together. But—" Bobbie looked her straight in the eye "—the time has come to quit cryin' in your beer—excuse me, your wine—and get on with your life."

"I'm trying, Bobbie. I really am."

"I know, sugar. You've just got to keep tryin'."

"It helps having a friend like you." Jesse sniffled back her tears and smiled tremulously. "Now, what do you think we ought to do until Hank gets here to drive you home?"

"I think we ought to finish this bottle and see who else we can find to talk about." Bobbie emptied the last of the wine into their glasses without spilling a drop—a considerable achievement, considering it was the next-to-the-last bottle. "Who do you want to trash next?"

Jesse sipped her wine and thought for a minute.

"You never did finish your story about that math teacher. What was his name—Will something—the guy who got fired?"

"Oh, yeah. William Duffy."

"If he didn't get in trouble for skinny-dipping with the gym teacher, why did Hank fire him?"

Bobbie never missed a beat.

"He had a drinking problem."

They had both exploded into gales of laughter. When Hank arrived an hour later, he glanced at them, then looked disapprovingly around the living room, focusing on the empty bottles lined up on the coffee table. The judgmental expression on his face set them both off into a fit of renewed giggles. Without a word, Hank had escorted his tipsy wife to their car, shaking his head. After they left, Jesse had gone up to bed with a smile on her face and slept like a rock, knowing she was very thoroughly smashed for the first time in her whole life, but rather liking the way it made her feel.

Now, having wakened to her first morning-after, Jesse clutched her queasy stomach as she carefully made her way downstairs to the front door. It had to be Bobbie, although she shouldn't be able to crawl this morning—if there was any justice in the universe.

The pounding on the door started up yet again. It couldn't be Bobbie. After last night, there was no way she could have the strength to knock that long or that loudly. A second, horrible thought entered her mind. What if it was Hank? She remembered the fate of Will something, the guy who had the drinking problem. Maybe Hank had come to give her her pink slip. He'd certainly looked disgusted enough last night to do it.

Raw pain shot through her temples, beating inside her head with each rap on the door. God, if he would stop that infernal noise, he wouldn't have to fire her. She would quit and make it easy for him. All she wanted was a quiet place to lie down and die. She stumbled to the door and opened it, only to stare in astonishment at the oddly familiar dark stranger who stood there, drenched and dripping, in the pouring rain.

ALL THE MONTHS HE'D planned this trip, Sloan had worried every detail over in his mind. He thought he was prepared for any eventuality. He was wrong.

He had driven toward this meeting with one thought, one concern: what would he say when he introduced himself? And how would Jesse react to having him turn up, unannounced, on her doorstep?

He had imagined shocked silence. He had prepared himself for tears and emotion. He had even considered the possibility that she might be bitter and angry at him.

It was pitch-black when he reached the city limits of Taos. When the thunderstorm started, it lashed the road with blowing, swirling sheets of water. Sloan had driven at a snail's pace, trying to keep his car on the unfamiliar road. He turned in at a truck stop and had breakfast, waiting until a decent hour before driving the three or four miles out to the Varner house.

Eight o'clock came and went without a sign of movement in the house. No lights came on. No curtains opened. Nothing. He sat in the car and listened to the rain. Maybe no one was home. There was a car in the garage, though, so he waited.

By nine o'clock he couldn't stand it any longer. He got out and dashed through the rain, seeking shelter under the wide overhang of the porch. He knocked and waited, turning his collar up against the blowing downpour. Assuming that the storm was drowning out the sound, he knocked again, louder and longer.

After a lengthy pause, he shrugged and gave up. He would go back to town and get a room at one of the hotels he'd passed, then call her later and set up a meeting. The long drive and sleepless night were getting to him, anyway. He turned and ran back to the car.

When the car door refused to open, it didn't take him long to figure out the problem. He cursed and wiped at the window in a futile attempt to clear off the rain. There were his keys, still dangling from the ignition.

He cursed again, eloquently. Of all the stupid, idiotic things to do. It was an old habit, locking his keys inside a car—so old that he had gotten pretty good at breaking into cars. All he needed was an old wire coathanger.

"You don't happen to have one in your back pocket, do you, hotshot?" he growled.

He braced his arms on the roof of the car and buried his head between them, stifling the urge to scream at the top of his lungs in pure frustration. Well, hell! This is what he deserved for driving all the way across the country on a fool's mission. He could have saved himself a lot of trouble by picking up the phone and talking to Jesse as any polite, sane person would have done. She probably wouldn't have wanted to see him, wouldn't want to stir up the memories again.

"You didn't want to hear that, did you, J. Sloan? That's why you didn't give her a chance to turn you down."

Despite the fact that he was already totally soaked, he shivered as a cold little river of rain took advantage of his bent head to wind its way inside his shirt collar and down his spine. He straightened and slicked his black hair straight back out of his eyes, wringing the water out with his fingers, squeegee-style. It helped for only a minute. He looked up at the dark morning sky. Judging from the mass of heavy clouds, the rain could go on for hours. With his luck, it could last for days.

"No use standing out here like a fence post. Let's knock one more time. If she doesn't answer, it's a long wet walk back to town."

He didn't really expect her to answer. It was possible she wasn't in there at all. Sloan took some of his frustration out on the massive door, slamming his knuckles against the hard wood with a vengeance. Suddenly the door swung open. Sloan stood frozen, one hand arrested in midknock, looking straight into Jesse Varner's sleepy brown eyes.

"Who are you?" she asked in a husky whisper. "What are you doing here?"

Sloan was silent for a long moment, even though he knew his silence frightened her. He couldn't help it. All he could do was look at her. She didn't look good—

No, that was the wrong way of putting it. She looked beautiful. Her hair was a wild, blond tangle. Her eyes were heavy-lidded and softly smudged with mascara. And she was obviously naked beneath the T-shirt that stopped just above her knees! Sloan looked back at her face, trying not to think about that.

She looked beautiful, but she also looked ill. Her skin was so pale beneath her tan that he was afraid she was about to pass out. She clutched at the door, wobbling slightly.

"I'm sorry, but I don't feel well," she said in a weak but impeccably polite voice. "Who—"

"If you aren't well, you don't need to be standing down here in the cold, half dressed."

She took a half step back, retreating from the rough rasp of his voice. He didn't mean to sound so harsh, but if she didn't have the sense to take care of herself, she needed someone to talk some sense to her.

"My name is Sloan Lassiter. I was a friend of your husband. May I—"

He didn't know whether it was the shock of his words or if she was really that ill, but at that moment, Sloan found himself reaching out to catch her as the last trace of color in her already pale cheeks blanched. Her lashes fluttered down and, without a sound, Jesse collapsed in a dead faint.

———

4

SLOAN LIFTED MICHAEL'S wife into his arms and stepped into the house, kicking the door shut behind him.

"If this isn't a hell of a note," Sloan swore as a crack of thunder exploded and lightning illuminated the dark interior of the house. "What am I supposed to do now, lady?"

Jesse remained still and silent in his arms—even when the cold drops of rain ran down from his face and landed on her T-shirt. Sloan noticed the way the wet fabric clung to her warm skin. He knew it was a rotten thing to stare, but he couldn't for the life of him tear his eyes away.

Bloody hell! Instead of taking care of her, instead of trying to find out what was the matter with her, all he could do was gawk at her like a sex-starved idiot!

"Damn it, Lassiter. What kind of pervert are you turning into, anyway?"

He shifted her limp form in his arms, trying not to notice the velvety texture of her skin where his fingers touched her. He wasn't trying to cop a feel, but as he held her, carefully supporting her hips and shoulders in his arms, there seemed to be an awful lot of bare skin everywhere he touched. Her brief sleep shirt had twisted and ridden up, exposing her long legs almost all the way to the apex of her thighs. And, it took all the self-control he could muster to look away from the gentle shifting of her breasts with each soft intake of air.

"Get a grip, man. This isn't an entry in a wet T-shirt contest. And it's not like you've never seen a pair of boobs before. Let's try to find the lady a place to lie down until we can figure out what's wrong with her."

Sloan shook his head, flipping back the shock of wet hair that hung down over his eyes, obscuring his vision. Despite the early-morning hour, the house was dark in the rainy gloom. For the first time, he was glad for the storm, blessing the uneven light given by the frequent bursts of lightning. He made his way carefully through the short entry hall and turned into the living room.

"Once I pull back the curtains and find the damned light switch, I'll get my head back on straight." Then, across the room, he noticed the outline of a sofa. "Just a second, Jesse. Let me get you comfortable and where I can take a clear look at you. Then I'll decide what needs to be done."

At the sound of his voice, Jesse gave a low-pitched groan and stirred in his arms. He was relieved that she was coming around. He'd been starting to worry that something might be seriously wrong. He remembered how Michael had drifted away, falling into ever-longer bouts of unconsciousness just before—

No! Sloan pushed away that thought, telling himself not to be a fool. He was overreacting. This was New Mexico, the good old U.S. of A., not that godforsaken corner of hell. There was help here—a doctor only a phone call away—if necessary. Not that there was anything to worry about, after all. He was sure there wasn't a real problem, but—

Hell, he wasn't going to jump to conclusions. All the same, he vowed, he was going to take good care of her.

He wasn't about to lose her now—not when he'd just found her.

He bent his head to brush his lips against her hair, moving carefully, with a touch so light he almost believed it was unintentional himself. She instinctively snuggled closer to the warmth of his body.

"Bobbie? Is that you?" Jesse's voice was a husky whisper. "I thought you went home last night."

"Sorry to disappoint you, but I'm not Bobby," Sloan said, his voice flat and hard. "My name is Lassiter, Ms. Varner. Sloan Lassiter. Do you remember?"

"It hurts my head to try to think," she complained, opening her eyes for a few seconds, looking up at him with a faint frown before her lids closed again. "When did Bobbie leave?"

"Your guess is as good as mine about that. I won't keep you up long, Ms. Varner. If you're feeling better now, I'll just borrow a hanger and be out of your way in a few minutes."

Yeah, that was a good plan. He was going to see that she was all right and then get out of here. The hell with the idea of talking to her calmly. One minute in the room with her had already convinced him that the smartest thing he could do was turn around and get out of town. One look at her and he realized his plan to see Michael's widow so that he could forget his fantasies was a washout.

Jesse moaned faintly, making his stomach knot at the sound of her pain.

"Are you feeling worse now?"

"I think I'm going to die."

"I don't think it's come to that yet," he said soothingly. "You just lie still a minute while I get the lights."

Sloan settled her on the couch, taking care to put a cushion under her head. She lifted one arm to cover her eyes.

"No lights, please. My head is splitting. Would you please get me a couple of aspirin from the kitchen?"

"We'll see about that in a minute. I don't think I should give you any medication until we see what's wrong. How long have you been sick? Do you need me to call your doctor?"

"I don't need a doctor. I need a couple of aspirin and a tall glass of water. My mouth is so dry."

"You don't seem to have a fever." He touched her cheek with the back of his hand, feeling only the cool smoothness of her skin. "I'll be back in just a minute."

He took a step backward and all hell broke loose. He bumped into a low table by the sofa, setting off a crashing of glass against wood. He spun around and caught a flash of movement. Even in the shadowy light he could make out the row of wine bottles careening and tumbling to the floor. His attempts to grab them were futile, and before he could get out of the way, the bottles were rolling about under and around his feet.

Sloan tried to move out of their way, but all he managed to do was add to the noise and confusion. His flailing feet made contact with one of the spinning bottles, sending it hurtling across the carpet like a glass missile. It scored a direct hit on the wall in its path, bursting into a shower of glistening shards on impact.

"What is going on?" Jesse sat up with a faint shriek. "Oh, my head!" She pressed the fingers of both hands to her temples.

"It's okay, Jesse." Sloan struggled to maintain his balance and to reassure her that he had the situation under control. "You just lie down and relax, and I'll take care of this mess."

She slowly sank back against the cushions and stared up at him, her fear apparent even in the dim light. She didn't know him from Adam. And the way he looked now, drenched to the skin and in the flickering electrical lighting, he could understand her dismay.

She was sick in the first place, and waking up to this chaos had to be scaring the hell out of her. He wasn't much to look at under normal circumstances, but wet and looming over her in the dark room, he knew he must look like a demon.

"You don't have to be afraid of me. I'm not nearly as bad as I look right now. Really."

Knowing how stern and threatening people always found him when he frowned, Sloan attempted a smile. He stepped back and his foot came down on another bottle. Losing his balance, he came tumbling forward on top of her.

With a superhuman effort, he managed to brace himself with his arms on either side of her to cushion the impact. He was partially successful, but there was no way to avoid the accident altogether.

Her arms had started up to ward off his fall. His body made contact with hers, and they came together with enough force to connect them from head to toe, but without the bone-jarring crunch he feared. And instead of holding him off, her arms opened as if to embrace him, and wound up around his shoulders, holding on for dear life.

They were both momentarily stunned and lay intertwined in an embrace as intimate as that of two lovers.

Sloan found himself staring down into the deepest brown eyes he'd ever seen. *Bedroom eyes.* That's what they were. He felt Jesse go rigid beneath him as she became aware of his sudden sexual arousal. She could hardly not notice it. He hadn't been with a woman in longer than he cared to think about. Being this close to the one woman who had been the focus of all his pent-up longings was creating a hunger he could neither control nor disguise.

His groin was pressed into the vee of her legs, the hard evidence of his desire separated from her body by only a few millimeters of cloth. When he attempted to lever himself up to take his weight off her, his pelvis tilted forward, pushing more directly against the flimsy barricade, grinding against her with unintentional insistence.

"No," she said raggedly. "Please. Just let me up."

Her words were a faint whimper, barely audible even this close. She removed her hands from where they had been clinging to his wide shoulders and wedged them between their bodies, pushing at him with a surprising strength. Sloan felt her trembling beneath him, shaking with an emotion that might have been fear.

Fear and something else: desire. She didn't expect to feel it, he was sure, but it was unmistakably there—that uninvited and reluctant longing. He could see it in the depths of her eyes, along with a flicker of panic that she was responding on such a basic level to him, a virtual stranger. And she *was* responding.

Sloan looked back into her eyes, to find her studying his face with shocked hunger.

She knew he saw her hunger. He would have had to be blind not to see the dark flush of humiliation that betrayed her. He tried to reassure her with a glance, wishing he could wipe away the guilty blush, but before he could say a word, Jesse broke the visual contact.

She clamped her lids shut and closed her teeth over her full lower lip, effectively stilling the giveaway trembling. She managed to make a low, pleading sob that begged him to end the physical closeness that was tormenting them both. He found her soft protest gave him the strength he needed to pull away from her.

"Jesse," he said softly, trying to ease the roughness from his voice, "I'm not going to hurt you. Give me the chance to get out of this with both of us having a shred of dignity left." Sloan then disentangled himself and stood on shaking legs. "Are you all right? Did I hurt you?"

"I'm fine," she said uncertainly. "Just let me lie here for a couple of minutes until my head stops swimming."

"Unless I miss my guess, you aren't going to feel much better until you get down some hot black coffee."

"Not yet," she groaned, raising her arm to cover her eyes. "I don't feel well enough to make it right now."

"Why don't you let me take care of the coffee while you take a shower and dress? Do you need any help getting to the bathroom?"

"Certainly not!" Jesse bristled at the suggestion. "I may be sick, but I'm not helpless."

She pulled herself up to a half-sitting position and glared at him. It was hard to suppress a grin at the sight of her trying to come across as being in control while she was still reeling.

"Look, you don't have to be embarrassed, Jesse," he said. "It's not a crime to have a hangover. I've had a few myself."

"I don't think you know me well enough to assume I've got a hangover, Mr.—"

"We don't need to stand on formalities, Jesse. Call me Sloan."

"It doesn't matter what I call you," she said, lifting a shaking hand to push her hair out of her eyes. "This is so embarrassing. You must think I'm some kind of a lush or—"

"Shh, Jesse," he murmured, wanting to comfort her now. "It doesn't matter what anyone thinks. Least of all, me."

"Especially you, Sloan Lassiter. I've been hoping to get a chance to meet you ever since I heard you were free. There's so much I wanted to ask you, to tell you, but—"

"But what?" He couldn't keep the slight tone of rebuke out of his voice. "Don't tell me you couldn't get in touch. No one else in the country has had any trouble finding me. I don't think you were at all interested in talking to me."

"That's not true." She flinched under his coolness. "It was just that...that finding you meant I had to come to grips with...well, with...everything else. I *do* want to be able to talk to you, but this isn't a good time for me. I really feel awful."

Jesse spoke so quietly he could barely hear her. She wasn't looking at him any longer, was just staring off into space as if she were seeing something, or someone else, far in the distance. Whatever she saw, it brought a liquid sheen to her eyes before she closed them.

All the anger drained out of him as suddenly as it had flared. There was something about this woman that made him lose control of himself. In the few minutes he had been with her, his emotions had run the gamut from hot to cold and back again. It wasn't a pleasant feeling, having someone able to bend him and move him so easily.

Sloan cursed silently, furious with himself for putting that withdrawn, hurt look on her face. And while she was sick, damn it. She was pale and the hollows under her eyes were even darker than a few minutes ago.

"Don't think about any of that now, Jesse. We can sort this out later. Right now, you need some strong, hot coffee and a long shower." He reached down and helped her to sit up. "I'm not used to thinking about anyone except myself lately, and it's made me even more of a selfish bastard than usual. Let's get you to the bathroom while I take care of making that coffee."

"I can get to the bathroom by myself, thank you." She bristled a bit and tried to shrug his hand off her arm. "If you'll move out of the way, I'll get up."

"I don't think that's such a good idea."

"Despite the evidence to the contrary, I'm not going to fall on my face again, Mr. Lassiter." She lifted her chin defiantly. "I'm doing fine now."

"You won't be so fine if you put your bare feet down on a piece of this broken glass." He kicked at a large piece of the shattered bottle, getting it out from under his feet. "Judging from the number of bottles rolling around the floor here, I'm surprised you managed to answer the door in the first place."

"Well, for heaven's sake, I didn't drink them all myself."

Sloan was only too aware of that fact. He had noticed every time she mentioned her friend, Bobby. He should have known she would have someone else in her life by now. Michael had been dead a long time, not even counting the months of separation that he'd been held captive.

No one could blame Jesse for having a life again, but Sloan didn't think much of a man who encouraged her to get bombed and then left her all alone to wake up in this condition.

"Mr. Lassiter?"

Her quizzical tone interrupted his thoughts.

"Sloan," he corrected automatically. "Sorry about the woolgathering. Time for you to get dressed—to get something warmer on," he amended, seeing her discomfort at his reminder of her scanty nightshirt. "Ready?"

He reached down and scooped her into his arms, not giving her a chance to object again. It took only a few steps to get away from the broken glass and reach the stairway landing. He stood her on the bottom step, holding on to her until she had a firm grip on the banister rail. When he was satisfied that her legs were going to support her, he stepped back and watched her make her wobbly way up the stairs.

"If you need any help, just yell and I'll come running."

"Thanks, but you've done more than enough. I can make it on my own from here."

"Sure, you can. Hurry, though. I don't like having breakfast all by myself."

He tried to keep his voice brisk and detached. It wasn't easy when he was battling the urge to carry her upstairs, but he knew she wouldn't appreciate any further interference. Her pride was already battered. He could see the effort it took to keep her back straight and her head up as she walked away.

The last thing he needed was an emotional attachment to Jesse Varner. She had been enough of a problem before he met her. He wasn't about to let her take over his reality—she already owned his dreams.

He remembered as clear as day the first time he had dreamed about her. Michael had spent an entire afternoon talking about nothing else. Sloan had been fed up with hearing her name. It was "Jesse did this" or "Jesse was wearing that," or "Then Jesse told me something or other." Sloan had lain back on his hard cot, tempted to put a pillow over his ears to block out the constant stream of Michael's chatter.

Instead he'd pretended to fall asleep. Finally, he'd actually drifted off into a restless half sleep where Michael's voice was only a distant, faintly irritating drone.

Then a strange thing had happened. It was as if he'd stepped into Michael Varner's rambling narrative, seeing himself acting out the stories as Michael related them. And in every scene there was Jesse. He could see her as a young woman, singing in the choir of her father's church, smiling at him as he sat, transfixed, in the front pew. The sun was streaming in through the stained-glass windows, filling the church with rose-tinted light. At that moment the whole world was peaceful and perfect, and at the center of the world was Jesse.

After the service he'd waited outside for her, leaning against the hood of his car, impatient for her to join him. She had come out the front door alone, looking like an angel, but there was a look of very human longing in her eyes as she approached him. Her choir robe was gone and the demure print dress she wore didn't hide her ripely curving body. Her blond hair bounced and shimmered in the sunlight as she ran down the steps toward him, calling his name.

"Sloan." Her voice was soft and warm. "Take me away from here, Sloan."

She'd held out her hand and he'd reached for her. At the instant their fingers should have met he'd wakened, jerking to a sitting position. After a moment of disorientation, he'd recognized the cell. Michael was still talking, softly now, half asleep himself, his mumbling still filled with Jesse's name. Then darkness had fallen and Michael had quietened into sleep. Sloan had been disgusted with himself. Wanting another man's wife—even in his dreams—made him feel like the lowest form of life.

He still felt that way, even if Jesse was Michael's widow now.

"Come on, Lassiter," he ordered. "Get a grip on yourself and find the kitchen. Make the coffee, get her sobered up, and get the hell out of here before it's too late."

He heard the sound of water running above his head, and his good intentions were cut dead. A sudden image of how Jesse would look naked made an instant lie of his pledge to get out while there was still time.

It was already too late. It had been too late for years.

5

JESSE PULLED A HEAVY, oversize sweater over her jeans. She had left her face free of makeup and tied her hair in a subdued ponytail at the nape of her neck. Even the gentle pressure exerted by the ribbon was almost more than she could stand. A quick shower and brushing her teeth had made her feel closer to human. Still, she was a long way from being able to cope with the man waiting downstairs.

J. Sloan Lassiter. She knew the name almost as well as she knew her own. Over the years she had come to think of them as almost a single entity—J. Sloan Lassiter and Professor Michael Varner, the two American hostages held somewhere in the Middle East, most probably Iraq.

When Jesse had heard on the nightly news that two Americans had been abducted, she had rushed over to turn up the sound, riveted to the television, listening intently for details. According to the special news bulletin, all that was known at first was that a group calling for a Pan-Arabic holy war had taken two men whom they were offering to release in exchange for two of their comrades being held in an American prison. A stern-looking official of the United States government had been interviewed and restated the long-standing policy of non-negotiation with terrorists. He'd promised further details regarding the hostages' identities as soon as that information was available.

Jesse had told herself not to panic. After all, there were hundreds of Americans traveling in the Middle East, and Michael wasn't important enough—at least to anyone but her—to be of any use as a bargaining chip. The incident did make her feel badly about their argument just before he left. She hadn't understood how he could go off and leave her for three weeks. He had accused her of being childish and selfish. She'd known he was right, but she had sulked about his trip for several days. They had made up, but Jesse had still felt abandoned.

She'd decided to call him at the hotel in Tel Aviv to apologize. The realization that something could happen to him had made all her complaints seem petty. When the concierge said that Michael had never checked in, Jesse had hung up the phone with trembling fingers and called her father.

Within hours, she had been contacted by three different agencies of the federal government who had asked all kinds of questions regarding the flight Michael had taken, names of people in the archaeology team, and any information she had about her husband's travel itinerary.

Jesse had answered the inquiries with as much patience as she could muster while fighting a growing feeling of dread. There was no way all these people would be putting so much energy into talking to her if they weren't certain Michael was in danger. By noon of the next day, her worst suspicions had been confirmed. The authorities had informed her that Michael and an oil-company negotiator named J. Sloan Lassiter were the two men who'd been taken hostage.

Jesse had found herself totally unable to cope for several weeks. Thank God she'd had her parents and

Michael's family to lean on. They had rallied around, giving her strength and encouragement. Her father had been solid as a rock, protecting her from the ensuing publicity and media attention that had threatened to rip her life apart. It seemed the whole world wanted pictures or an interview with her—even a network news show had called, wanting her to appear on their program. Reverend Green had fielded the reporters' questions, stepping in and making sure Jesse had the solitude she needed to come to grips with her grief. After several weeks, another crisis had taken over the headlines, and the constant requests had dwindled to an occasional inquiry.

After the initial shock about Michael's kidnapping had dulled, Jesse had held on to the myth that Michael was safe with an unshakable fervor until the day had come when the terrorists announced that Michael was dead.

It had taken her a long time to forgive J. Sloan Lassiter for daring to survive.

The man she had just left downstairs was very much alive, bursting with vitality and strength. For a few seconds he appeared to be the dark stranger of her dreams come to life; then she recognized him from the newspaper photographs—J. Sloan Lassiter in the flesh.

The hangover and the storm must have muddled her senses. How else could she confuse the two? No wonder she had fainted. Of all the men on earth to fantasize about, Sloan Lassiter was last on her list. She couldn't think of him without thinking of Michael—of Michael's death.

She retrieved her sneakers from under the bed, refusing to let herself dwell on that subject. It had taken her months to be able to get through a whole day without thinking about it, without seeing a dozen horrible variations of what he must have suffered through before the end.

The terrorists had never revealed the details of Michael's death. Instead, they had issued a statement announcing that one of the American "imperialists" had died during captivity. It wasn't until weeks later that Michael was declared dead.

"And now," Jesse muttered half aloud, "J. Sloan Lassiter himself is sitting in my kitchen, drinking my coffee. I'd better get down there and see what he came here for."

She stepped out into the hall, closing the bathroom door behind her carefully. When she was halfway down the stairs, the distinctive aroma of freshly brewed coffee assaulted her nostrils.

It was all she could do not to turn and bolt back upstairs to the bathroom. Normally, coffee was the first thing she thought of in the morning, but today her stomach was unconvinced. Slowly, with hesitant and cautious steps, she made her way to the kitchen, stopping just at the doorway to watch Sloan Lassiter for a moment before he became aware of her presence.

He looked surprisingly at home in her tiny, efficient kitchen. The wet-seal blackness of his hair had dried to a dark mahogany brown, showing reddish highlights. He had taken off his rain-soaked jacket and rolled up the sleeves of the light blue cotton shirt beneath it. His jeans still weren't dry and they looked uncomfortably cold as they clung to his hips and thighs.

Jesse tried not to notice the taut firmness of his rear end, but the damp fabric couldn't help but showcase his assets, and hangover or no, she was only human. With a concerted effort, she turned her attention elsewhere.

In addition to starting the coffee maker, he had opened a can of frozen orange juice and was trying to dig the solid block out with a spoon. Jesse smiled, amused by the intensity he brought to the small task. He chipped at the contents in silence for a few seconds before plunking the can down and tossing the now bent spoon into the sink where it landed with a sharp metallic ring.

"Take it easy, Mr. Lassiter," she said in a loud stage whisper. "My head is only in slightly better shape than that spoon."

"I can straighten both problems, if you give me just a minute."

He reached into the sink and picked up the spoon. She watched as he held the shiny metal in his hands and reversed the curve in the handle, restoring the original shape in a second's time. He smoothed the straight line of the handle between his thumb and forefinger before placing it back in the sink, so gently that it didn't make a sound.

Then Sloan turned and faced her, giving her a thorough but nonleering once-over as she stood clinging to the door frame. Jesse knew she looked better than a while ago, but her self-confidence was still somewhere between low and zero. It was bad enough to be in this condition without having it witnessed by a virtual stranger—especially this particular stranger.

"Now, about your head . . ." He picked up the juice can and eyed it doubtfully. "The first step in the treatment is vitamin C. We really ought to start with this, but in the interests of saving time, have you got a can of tomato juice stashed anywhere?"

"I don't mean to be a grouch after everything you've done, but could we start with a jolt of caffeine and a couple of aspirin and work our way up to the juice?"

"Not a good idea. You don't want to shock your stomach with all that hot, bitter stuff first. It might throw it right back at you."

"You sound like an expert on the subject, Mr. Lassiter."

"Sloan," he corrected absently as he rummaged through a cabinet of canned goods. "Enough of an expert to know what works. Ah, here it is."

He focused his attention on assembling a variety of items on the counter near the tall glass already sitting on the counter. Jesse watched as he opened the refrigerator and delved inside, bringing out an assortment of things including Worcestershire sauce, Tabasco sauce, a lemon, and a carton of eggs. Her stomach lurched at the thought of smelling eggs cooking.

"If you're considering making omelets, count me out. I'll just grab a cup of coffee and take my chances that my stomach will be forgiving."

"Don't worry. I'm not going to start cooking." He gave her a grin so lopsided it looked as if he was out of the habit of smiling. "As green as you were earlier, I didn't figure the smell of food would be in either of our best interests."

"Thank heavens, a perceptive man!"

"At your service, ma'am."

Jesse stepped closer to him, trying to see what he was mixing and shaking and putting so much energy into making. For a man who had forsworn cooking, he was sure messing up a lot of dishes.

"If you'll let me get my aspirin, I'll get out of your way while you finish your breakfast...or whatever that is."

"Oh, it's not for me. I ate hours ago."

Sloan held a large glass of murky red liquid up between him and the light, examining its color as if inspecting priceless rubies. It looked like... Well... it looked awful. Jesse shook her head.

"If it's not for you, I hope you don't think I have any intention of drinking it."

"I wish you'd at least give it a chance, Jess," he said reasonably. "It's a surefire cure for what ails you right now."

"The main thing that's *ailing* me right now is the thought of getting within arm's length of that stuff." She wrinkled her nose in disgust. "What all did you put in there, anyhow?"

"Sorry, I can't tell you that without seeing your clearance dossier, ma'am. Matter of national security, you understand." The smile was wider this time, almost natural looking. "This little formula..." He sniffed the mixture, then shook in another generous dollop of hot pepper sauce. "As I was saying, this very formula has saved more American lives than penicillin."

"I still think I'll pass, thank you."

"You can have a cup of that nasty black coffee as a chaser," he promised reasonably. "Just a couple of big gulps and it will be all gone. You really will feel lots better, I promise."

Since Jesse was feeling more awful by the minute, she decided to take his chances on the offer. She reached out and took the glass from his outstretched hand.

"If this makes me any sicker than I already am, you're going to be facing homicide charges." She took a deep breath and lifted the glass nearer to her lips. "Down the hatch, right?"

"Right."

She had touched the edge of the rim to her lips when he grabbed her hand. His grip was firm, stopping her before she had even a tiny taste, and his fingers were noticeably hot against her skin.

"I almost forgot the magic ingredient. Shut your eyes."

"If I'm not mistaken, that's an egg in your hand. This gunk looks bad enough. There's no way you can make me drink raw egg."

"You won't even know it's in there if you just drink it down fast." Sloan cracked the shell on the edge of the glass and the egg slipped beneath the surface with scarcely a plop. He gave her fingers a pat that was meant to be encouraging, but which only focused her attention on how gentle his hands were, despite their strength.

"It won't be as bad as it sounds, Jesse. You won't even taste it."

"No way, Mr. Lassiter. I may be hung over, but I'm not totally without a functioning brain."

She wasn't sure about that. At the moment her brain seemed to have turned to mush. She was barely able to hold her head up or walk straight, and yet all she could focus on were the few centimeters of skin resting under Sloan Lassiter's fingertips.

"Trust me."

"That line hasn't worked since the Boston Strangler," she said sharply, knowing that she was overreacting because of her uncomfortable physical awareness of him. "Give me one reason why I should trust you."

There was a long pause. He didn't move his hand from hers, but his fingers were suddenly cold. She felt the warmth drain out of him like lifeblood, leaving his face the color of ashes. All the teasing was gone from his voice, and the glint of laughter was missing from his eyes.

"I told your husband I'd take care of you. I intend to keep my word. It would make things easier if you would cooperate, just a little."

Jesse hated seeing him like this. It bothered her to admit to herself that she had such a strong reaction to his emotional state, one way or another. After only an hour's exposure to Sloan Lassiter, she had realized he was a very complicated man. He had come in with a major strike against him—he had made it home and Michael hadn't. However, there was something about him that intrigued her. He could be surly and judgmental one moment, then as charming and lighthearted as an old friend the next.

There was a great deal of pain dammed up behind his eyes. Jesse didn't understand why it hurt her so much to know that. Suddenly she knew that there was almost nothing she wouldn't do to make his hurt go away. It didn't make a lot of sense, given the circumstances. No matter. This was one time she wasn't going to fight her instincts.

"You're right. I am being uncooperative." She was rewarded by a slight relaxation in his stiff posture. "After you've been so kind, the least I can do is try your magic potion. It can't make me feel much worse." She took one last glance at the concoction and suppressed a shudder of revulsion. "Here goes."

With a silent prayer that she wouldn't disgrace herself by upchucking on his shoes before she got it down, Jesse scrunched her eyes shut, held her breath, and vowed to drink as much as she could hold. She tipped back her head and swallowed.

Much to her surprise, it wasn't half bad. The fiery Tabasco and the tangy bite of the Worcestershire sauce hid whatever else the mixture contained. She stopped and took another breath, then decided to try a little more.

She opened her eyes and found that she had already finished half of it. At the same moment she noticed that the faint queasiness that had plagued her stomach was already receding. Sipping cautiously, she drank until she spotted the egg resting on the bottom of the glass, still whole and staring up at her with its unblinking yellow eye. She looked up at Sloan and set the glass down on the counter.

"There's no way on earth I'm going to swallow that egg," she said defiantly. "If you want to get mad again, go ahead. Just give me my coffee and get on with your tantrum."

"You did great," he said quietly. "And I didn't mean to come down so hard on you. I've just been kind of moody lately. Ignore it."

His mouth quirked up at one corner and he didn't look so forbidding anymore. He stepped closer and led her to a chair at the table. The touch of his hand at her elbow was polite and perfectly proper, but it made Jesse nervous. She sank down into the chair, grateful for the support for her shaking legs. When Sloan moved away from her and walked back to the counter, she tried to figure out what was going on here.

She watched him as he reached into the cabinet and took down a couple of mugs. The fabric of his shirt pulled across the width of his shoulders and emphasized the strong muscles underneath. His body tapered to emphasize narrow hips and well-developed legs.

Jesse caught herself staring at his rear end again and ordered her eyes to look elsewhere.

Good Lord, what kind of sex-starved creature was she turning into? A man like this doubtless had a dozen lady friends on his string. He probably had to beat them off with a stick. How embarrassed would he be to pay a visit to a friend's widow and find her staring lustfully at his butt?

Face it, Jesse, she warned herself silently. *You have been alone too long.* She mentally scolded herself for having such thoughts.

"Are you ready to try this now?"

Jesse jumped slightly, pulled out of her reverie by Sloan's arrival with a steaming mug of aromatic coffee. She inhaled the rising vapors and took a cautious sip.

"Mmm. This is perfect. Just the way I like it. Lots of cream and no sugar." She looked up at him curiously. "How did you know?"

"You'd be surprised at the things I know about you, Jesse."

"Oh, really? Such as?"

"That you wear a size-nine shoe."

"Eight and a half," she corrected.

"No, a size nine. You just *buy* an eight and a half." He watched her sipping her coffee, glad to see a bit of color coming back into her cheeks. "I heard all about your old boyfriends."

"Then you should know that I never even went out with another boy besides Michael."

"Except for Aaron King."

"That wasn't a real date," she objected. "Aaron was captain of the football team and I was—"

"Homecoming queen."

"Michael told you about that?" Sloan nodded and she went on. "That night was the first time Michael kissed me. Really kissed me, I mean."

"Under the bleachers in the gym."

"My goodness. You do know all my secrets. I hope you aren't into blackmail."

"It wouldn't do me any good if I were. According to Michael, you never did a bad thing in your whole life."

"He always was pretty good at making excuses for me." Jesse didn't feel much like teasing anymore. "I don't think many people are lucky enough to have one person who knows every bad thing about them and still loves them so totally."

"He did love you, Jesse. More than anything. We talked about just about everything under the sun, but for Michael all topics eventually led back to you. Toward the end—"

Jesse couldn't help the faint gasp that escaped her lips at hearing him discussing his final days with Michael. Sloan flushed dark with embarrassment and bit out an apology.

"God, I'm sorry, Jesse." He took a couple of steps backward. "I didn't mean to bring any of that up. Hell, I shouldn't have come here in the first place." He looked tormented. "I thought I could do this, but it's all wrong. I—"

He spun on his heel and turned his back to her, standing as still and quiet as a statue. Jesse knew he didn't want her to witness his struggle to mask his raw, naked pain—the same kind of pain she felt all too frequently.

"You don't know what it was like." His voice was thick, almost hoarse. "We were like brothers— No, like parts of each other . . . trying to get by, holding on to whatever little pieces of our lives we could . . . talking to keep our lives from being just memories. Michael talked about you and . . ." He bent his head and made a strangled sound.

She understood then, in a flash of insight, why he had come. It went beyond devotion to a fallen comrade. It was more than making good on a deathbed promise. Sloan Lassiter had loved Michael, and was suffering his loss as much as she was.

Without thinking of anything more than comforting him, she went to stand behind him and reached out to lay her hand gently on his shoulder. It was like touching a chunk of living marble. He didn't pull away exactly, but he stilled and his breathing became shallow and rapid.

"It's all right, Sloan," she said. "I want you to talk to me about Michael."

"You don't need me to tell you about him. He always said you knew him better than anyone else in the world."

"He *was* my world," Jesse said simply. "I want you to tell me about what happened to him. How . . ." She swallowed hard. "How did he die?"

"No. You don't need to hear about it. Not from me."

"I *do* need to hear about it. Especially from you."

"Let it go, Jess. It's all in the past. Let it stay there."

"I can't. Don't you understand that? Until I hear, until I can sort it all out in my mind, I'll never be able to let it go. And you have to help me."

"I don't have to do anything," he snapped. "I've already lived through it once. You don't have any idea what you're asking, to make me go through it all again."

"You're right, Sloan. I don't know what happened, but I have a right to know." She was being cruel to ask him to open the barely healed wounds, but he was her last link to Michael.

"Maybe I don't have any right to ask it of you, but no one else was there, and I have to know." She dug her fingers into the hardness of his shoulder. "Look at me, please."

For a moment she thought that he would ignore her plea, but slowly he gave in to the insistent pressure of her fingers and allowed himself to be tugged around to face her. He was evidently as affected as she by the sudden flare of emotion.

"This isn't going to do either of us any good, Jesse. I should leave now."

"No, don't go," she begged. "Stay and help me. It will do you some good to talk about him with me. Let's help each other. You don't know all the nights I've spent thinking about it...all the days trying to imagine what Michael was thinking about...if he was in pain..."

"Can't you just remember him the way he was? Reality isn't always better than nightmares, Jess."

"I'm strong. I can deal with reality," she promised, biting the tender flesh inside her cheek to keep her composure. "It's just that I don't have anything to put at the end."

Her voice broke, and the pent-up tears started against her will. "You don't know how many nights I've spent trying to tell myself to put it behind me and get on with my life. What no one seems to understand is..." She was crying in earnest now, shaking with the force of her sobs. "Until I say goodbye to Michael, it will never be over for me. Never."

When he held out his arms, Jesse accepted the haven of his protection and burrowed into the strength of his embrace. She felt the scalding wetness of his tears mingling with her own and felt the heaves of silent grief racking his body, and to comfort him, she wrapped her arms around him in return. They stood together and wept for the man they both loved, the sounds of their grief muffled by the falling rain.

6

IT WAS A STUPID THING to do.

Sloan knew it from the moment he reached out to hold her, but there was no power on heaven or earth that could have stopped him from taking Jesse into his arms. She seemed so afraid, so lonely; so very lost, that he would have risked anything to protect her.

Her tears were coming in fits and starts like those of an overtired child. His own loss of control had been brief, but cathartic. He couldn't remember the last time he had cried. Not when his father had died. Not even when the guards had come in and dragged out Michael's lifeless body with such callous indifference.

The most amazing thing about it was that he didn't feel any shame. For a man who had spent his whole life trying to weed out any hint of emotional weakness, he had, without embarrassment, blubbered like a snot-nosed kid in front of a woman he wanted.

And he did want Jesse. That was the real problem. He could handle the idea of looking after her interests and sobering her up and feeling protective. No sweat. He could carry out a friend's last wish of looking in on his widow. Those were noble and honorable intentions; no one could fault him for that. But—he savored for a moment the sensation of holding Jesse in his arms—the time had come to get a grip on this situation before it got out of hand.

"Come on, honey," he said. "Your coffee is going to get cold."

She sniffled a couple of times and then raised her head to look at him. Damn, even with swollen eyes and a red nose, she took his breath away! This wasn't how he had imagined holding her. The Jesse of his dreams had never looked anything other than perfect. Sloan had never imagined her tearstained and messy. And he was as taken with her now, in the all-too-human condition of grief, as he had been with his dream woman.

It was damn frustrating and confusing as hell, this attraction to the flesh-and-blood Jesse. Sloan didn't know quite what to do about the situation. The one thing he was sure of, though, was that as long as he held her like this, he wasn't going to be able to think straight at all.

"Come on, Jesse," he said, clearing his dry throat. "Hush, now."

Sloan gently disentangled them both from each other's arms, careful not to make her feel awkward about it.

"Why don't you go wash your face and let me get you a fresh cup and maybe a slice of toast?"

"You'll stay for a while, then?"

"Yeah, I'll be here. Now, go."

The smile she gave him was the first ray of sun he'd seen the whole damned day, and he returned it. Not until she had been gone for several seconds did it come to him that he was still smiling.

"Stupid bastard," he chided himself. "Next thing you know, you'll be buying her a corsage and asking her to the senior prom."

He poured the lukewarm coffee down the sink and rinsed the mug, setting it beside the pot until she got back. For lack of anything better to do, he decided to give the orange juice another shot. It was still frozen, but with a little elbow grease, he managed to coax it out of the can and into the pitcher he had found in the cabinet next to the glasses.

"A regular Betty Crocker, aren't you, Lassiter?" he asked as he found half a loaf of bread and popped a couple of slices in the toaster. "If you keep this up, you may not have to go out looking for work at all. The lady of the house might hire you on as her chief cook and bottle washer."

"That's not a bad idea. Can you actually cook?"

Sloan whirled around to see Jesse standing just behind him, smiling. She appeared calmer, though her eyes were still a little puffy.

"Can I cook?" he asked incredulously. "Can Wayne Gretsky play hockey? Can Ella Fitzgerald sing the blues? Can Mark Spitz do the backstroke?"

"Mark who?"

"The generation gap rears its ugly head," he muttered half seriously. "Just sit down and I'll get your breakfast."

He edged the conversation away from anything heavy, telling himself she needed to eat in peace. Besides, a world-class hangover deserved some respect, and from all indicators, the lady had been hitting in the major leagues. He was amazed to discover that if it took a little clowning around to make her feel better, he was ready to put on baggy pants and floppy shoes. For a man who had the reputation of being a hard ass, the realization came as quite a shock.

Jesse took a couple of bites of toast. She tasted the coffee and rewarded him with a satisfied sigh.

"My compliments to the chef. You really *can* cook."

"Slapping a little butter and jam on toast isn't too much of a challenge. Of course, I can cook. Don't you know that bachelors would starve to death if they didn't learn to make breakfast and grill a steak?"

"My experience with bachelors is somewhat limited. Isn't there always take-out pizza and chicken? And frozen dinners?" she added. "They make some very good frozen dinners these days."

"Most people don't live like that, Jesse. Just because you can't boil water—"

He stopped midsentence, remembering how Michael had laughed about her escapades in the kitchen. Sloan had thought then that a woman who looked like Jesse could get away with burned toast. She was looking at him over the rim of the mug as she sipped.

"How would you know a thing like that?"

"You have too much enthusiasm for TV dinners." Sloan watched her face to see how she took the evasion. Not that well, judging from the look on her face. "No one who could cook at all would eat that frozen cardboard."

Oh, hell, Lassiter. How many times are you going to put your foot in it today? She was still watching him, those velvety brown eyes silently accusing him of lying. *Give me a break, sweetheart. I don't want to get into all this now.*

"It was just a lucky guess," he amended, searching for a way out of his blunder. "That, and the little excursion I took through your pantry. There's not enough real food in this kitchen to make a single meal, but you've got enough junk food squirreled away to last out a siege."

"Sherlock Holmes would be proud of that kind of logic."

There was more than a hint of sarcasm in her voice. And, although she didn't force the issue, he could see that she wasn't buying his story. Acting more out of instinct than anything else, he faced her head-on. He crossed his arms over his chest and leaned back against the wall, watching her until she flushed under his scrutiny and looked away. Whether the rush of color in her cheeks came from anger or embarrassment, he wasn't sure, but it was a definite improvement to be on the intimidating side of the confrontation, for a change.

"Aren't you going to have something? Not even coffee?" she asked.

"Not right now." He looked down at his watch, unable to face her accusatory stare for much longer. "At the risk of being cute, do you think I could take a rain check on the offer? And maybe borrow a hanger from you?"

"A hanger?"

"Yeah, a wire hanger. I locked my keys in the car."

"You know how to open the door with a hanger?" She brightened a bit, flexing her shoulders and sitting up straighter in the chair. "I always wanted to see someone do that. Can I watch?"

Sloan tried not to notice how the movement outlined the thrust of her breasts underneath the sweater. For God's sake, she was only trying to get comfortable and here he was, staring at her like a lecherous old man. Yeah, it was way past time to get out of here.

"I think your education in breaking and entering will have to wait." He glanced out the window, then shook his head. "It's still pouring down out there. No sense in both of us getting soaked."

"There's no sense in either of us getting soaked," she corrected. "Chances are, your car will still be there when the rain stops. We're pretty far off the beaten path out here for anyone to steal it. And after all, it is locked."

"So, it is," Sloan acknowledged her teasing with a faint shrug. "The way it looks, I may need an ark to get out of here. I'd wear out my welcome long before forty days and nights were up, so I might as well get a move on before that driveway of yours turns into a swamp."

"It's probably too late for that. All it takes is a light shower and I'm in mud up to my hubcaps." Jesse got up and walked over to stand beside him, close enough for him to smell the soapy freshness of her skin. "Besides, why are you in such a hurry? Surely you didn't drive all the way out here to turn around and leave before we even have a chance to talk."

"I'm not much of a talker. I just came by to see how you were doing. I promised..." Sloan found he couldn't get the words out. He couldn't bring himself to say Michael's name to her. "I promised your husband that I'd check in on you...kind of see that you were being taken care of."

Jesse's expression became wistful when he brought up the subject of Michael. He had to curl his hands into fists at his sides in order not to embrace her.

God, how he wanted to help her! More than anything, he wanted to make the hurt go away for her, even if he could never forget it himself. She needed to be comforted, to be held; but he sure as hell wasn't the man for the job.

His whole life was a testimony to just how unprepared he was to hold on to anything or anybody. From the time he was born he had been dragged all over the world, from one military base to the next. His family had moved so much, he'd never even had a dog to practice hanging on to, much less a long-term girl-friend. As soon as he got interested in one, Uncle Sam would issue transfer papers and it was time to pull up stakes again. He learned quickly that it hurt less if he didn't get too involved. Except for a few short-lived affairs, he had remained unattached over the years.

There had never really been a woman he couldn't live without—starting with his mother. Sheila Lassiter had been a pretty, vivacious woman, the type who needed laughter and parties, not the straight-and-narrow existence of a career officer's wife. She had gotten her fill of the regimented life of the Army when Sloan was just a boy. She left when he was barely ten, swearing tear-fully that she knew he would be better off with his fa-ther. Sloan remembered her vows of love and concern, but he had never been able to shake the feeling that what she really wanted was to be rid of the responsi-bility of a family in general and him in particular.

Colonel Lassiter had handled her departure stoi-cally—the way he handled everything else. Sloan tried to imitate his father's attitude and succeeded—at least, to all outward appearances. When his mother died in a car wreck when he was fifteen, Sloan stood dry-eyed at her funeral. The colonel had been proud of him then. After all, expressing emotion too openly was a sign of weakness, wasn't it? he thought bitterly.

Despite his efforts to please his father, they had never forged any close bond except a wary kind of respect for each other. Still, it had been a real blow when his fa-ther had died in Vietnam. But Sloan had denied his sense of loss in the way he'd been taught and become even more of a loner after that.

Of course, there had been his friendship with Mi-chael—that had been special without question—yet even that friendship had come about largely as a result of circumstances. If they hadn't been literally locked up and kept in each other's pockets for so long, Sloan had no doubt that he would have escaped—as usual—by keeping the kid at a distance.

Still, the bond had existed, regardless of how it happened. He had held on to Michael at the end, trying to keep him from giving up, and look how much good that had done.

For a month Michael had been sick, starting with what seemed to be a simple cold. But the cold had worsened and a lingering fever had set in. Sloan had lain in bed night after night, listening with a heavy heart to Michael's bouts of coughing, which left him weak and pale. He had tried to reduce the fever by sponging Michael with a torn strip of cloth wet with part of their ration of drinking water, cursing the inadequacy of his makeshift treatment.

The guards had remained silent and unresponsive as always, ignoring Sloan's demands for a doctor or some kind of medicine. On one occasion Sloan lost his temper and grabbed one of the guards in a desperate effort to force some kind of response. All he had gotten was a crack across the skull with the butt of a rifle that left him crumpled on the floor and two days without rations of food.

Sloan drew his thoughts back from that terrible night and looked at Michael's wife. Could Jesse really handle the details of Michael's death? She seemed so emotionally fragile and not quite prepared to let go of Michael.

"You aren't going to leave right away, are you?" Her question wasn't quite a plea, but he saw the panic flutter across her face, and knew it had cost her to ask it.

"I want to have the chance to get to know you a little. There are so many things I want to ask—things no one but you can tell me about Michael, so many questions—"

"I didn't come here to be interrogated."

As soon as the words were out of his mouth, he regretted his curtness. Jesse was obviously hurt by the venom in his voice; he could see it in the faint pink flush of embarrassment on her high cheekbones. Damn, the last thing he wanted to do was make her any more uncomfortable than she already was.

"Sorry, Jesse. I didn't mean to be so abrupt. It's just that I've answered so many questions since I got out— doctors, government agents, reporters—everyone I've seen has a list of questions."

"I don't want to push you. And I do know how you feel. I thought for a while I'd go crazy from all the busybodies. You don't owe me any answers."

"It's not that I don't want to give them to you. That's part of why I came here—to talk to you." He cleared his throat. "You, of all people, have the right to ask me anything, but . . ." He hesitated, not knowing how to make her understand how hard it was for him to talk about Michael. "I'm not good with words. Michael always said it was like pulling teeth to get two sentences out of me."

"I'm surprised you ever got a chance to say that much with Michael around." She smiled, remembering, inviting him to share the remembrance. "He loved to talk, didn't he?"

"Yeah. Sometimes I wished he would shut up, but if he had, I expect I would have gone crazy."

"I know. I still wake up sometimes at night, thinking I've heard his voice. There were times before he died . . . times when I could almost swear he was in the next room. I guess I wanted it so much, my imagination ran away with me."

The loss and longing and love in her voice irritated him even as he felt the same emotions.

"Maybe you were dreaming, but halfway across the world, he was probably saying your name. He talked about you all the time."

It was true, but he hated telling her in a way. Somehow, watching the emotions filter across her face when he told her about Michael made him feel more desolate than he had when he sat alone in that barren little room. At least there, his imagination could let him believe that Jesse was his. This Jesse belonged to the real world; and in her heart, she still belonged to Michael.

"He talked about you so much, I felt I knew you— you and his parents. I kind of adopted you all in my mind." Sloan stopped short of telling her how completely he had been taken over by Michael's family in general and by her in particular. "The last thing he said was how much he loved you."

"My poor, sweet Michael." Her eyes glistened once more with tears—the same tears that choked her throat so much, her voice was nearly inaudible. "Oh, God, how I wish I could have been with him . . . to hold him. He shouldn't have been alone."

"I wish he had been with you, too, but he wasn't *all* alone," Sloan offered, wishing he had more comfort to give. "I was there, holding him."

"What happened, exactly? All I heard was that he probably caught some kind of virus."

"Pneumonia, I think. I'm not a doctor. I begged them to get a doctor for him, but the damn bastards wouldn't give us so much as an aspirin."

"He was in pain, then?"

Sloan looked down at her white, pinched face. *Good work, Lassiter. Didn't you just admit that she's not ready to hear how bad it was. She's hurting enough without you playing it all out for her to hear.* He tried to soften the horrible truth.

"I made him as comfortable as I could, Jess. I think by the end he was just tired of fighting." That wasn't much help, judging by the way her face blanched. "Are you going to pass out on me again?" She shook her head, but he wasn't convinced. "Come on. You'd better sit down."

"I don't need to sit down. I need to know what happened. How long—"

"For the love of God, Jesse. There are some questions you shouldn't ask. Sometimes it's better to just accept, without knowing too much."

He tried to give the impression of looking at her without actually making eye contact. If he got caught in those tormented eyes, he wasn't sure he would be able to walk out of here. There was no sense in getting more tangled up in her life. So far, she didn't know how crazy she made him feel, how raw and hungry he was for a taste of all the things he had only dreamed about.

"Would you look at me, please?" she begged. "Just look at me, so I can get through to you."

"Don't make this hard on both of us, Jesse." He continued to stare at a spot just over her right shoulder, hating the hoarse edge in his voice as he avoided granting her request.

"I shouldn't have come here at all, you know. I'm not cut out for this kind of stuff."

"Not cut out for what?"

She put one hand on his cheek, turning his face to meet her gaze. Her touch was light, but he felt the pressure of each finger on his skin, and he drew back, flinching as if he were scorched by fire. Yet, even the pain of the contact was less than the pleasure of having her hand against his flesh.

"Would you give me a break?"

"I'm sorry. All I want is to hear about my husband. Can't you take a couple of hours to talk to me?"

"Sorry. I'm getting kind of tired of talking."

Sloan stepped away from her and strode to the window, glaring at the leaden clouds. His spirits were as gray as the weather.

"Look, lady! I don't mean to sound like a complete bastard, but I only came to say hello and pay my respects. I spent eighteen months of my life nursemaiding your husband. I didn't mind that, but to tell you the truth, I don't relish the idea of telling you all the gory details and watching as you wallow in self-pity for the next two hours. I don't get off on telling maudlin stories to a neurotic drunk."

"That's an awful thing to say! And I've never been drunk in my life," she said, her eyes snapping with righteous anger. "That is, except for last night."

"Yeah, and I was lucky enough to arrive just in time for the big event. Is that how the story goes?"

He hated playing games with her, but he didn't have much of a choice right now. It was safer than having her know he believed her story. They would both be better off if she saw him as a coldhearted cynic instead of a sympathetic well of stories about her late husband. Sloan smarted under the withdrawal of her good graces. It seemed wiser though, to cut the tenuous ties now.

"You may not believe it, but that's exactly the truth."

"Whatever you say, Ms. Varner. But if this is your first time, for an amateur you sure managed to make a good start. I picked up at least four bottles in there. I don't think I could have handled that much myself, and I've had more than a little practice."

"Not that it's any of your business, but I didn't drink it all by myself. My friend Bobbie—"

"Ah, yes. I believe you did mention your friend before. He isn't much of a gentleman to leave you in the condition I found you in."

Sloan didn't like the sharp twist of discomfort he felt just under his ribs at the idea of her and the mysterious Bobby. He didn't even like the knowledge that she had belonged to Michael; but the notion of her guzzling wine with some rednecked cowboy set his teeth on edge. Still, unpleasant as it was, the gut-wrenching reaction did make it easier to keep baiting her.

"I don't think you have sterling credentials for judging gentlemanly behavior yourself, Mr. Lassiter," she said scornfully. "It may not have been included in your upbringing—" she made the word sound as if she was sure he'd never had any "—but it's really bad manners to come into someone's home, uninvited, and pass judgment on their behavior."

"Uninvited?" Sloan had meant to rile her yet the accusation made him strike back, hitting a little harder than he ever intended. "You open the door wearing damned little more than perfume and a smile and fall into my arms, and I'm accused of coming in without an invitation?" He gave a bitter snort that fell short of laughter. "Seems to me I either had to accept that as an invitation or step out of the way and watch you smack your face on the ground."

"Since I didn't have any choice in the matter, I guess I have to thank you for catching me." She didn't look particularly grateful, but she did get the words out. "Thank you."

"You're quite welcome, lady," he said, admiring her dignity. She lifted her chin and faced him with a haughty grace, proud even when forced to concede. "Knowing how badly you hate to admit you're wrong, I appreciate the effort, Jesse."

"No, don't do that," she said in a ragged whisper. "Please, just don't do that again."

She wasn't angry with him anymore. All the fight had suddenly gone out of her. There was fear in her eyes now. She didn't move at all physically, but as Sloan watched, she pulled back from him and stared at him, horror-stricken.

"For God's sake, Jesse. What's the matter?"

"It's not fair." Her voice was a dry husk of itself. "I don't know anything, and you know so much. You have everything. It's not fair."

"What are you talking about? What do I know? What do I have?"

Jesse sat back down in the chair and clutched the edge of the table so hard her knuckles were white. Her face was pale as death, and he really was afraid she was going to faint again. He started toward her, but she stopped him with a word.

"Michael."

Sloan froze, stopping dead in his tracks.

"You know so much about me. How I like my coffee. About my awful cooking. And my temper." She said the one word that stood between them like an eternal monolith. "Michael. It was him. He told you all about me, about our life. You were with him at the end, not me. You have everything."

Only two steps separated them, but it might have been a thousand miles. After all the months of wishing to be with her and hating himself for wishing, Jesse was right with him, close enough for him to touch, but he might as well have remained in that one-room cell. All she wanted from him was his memories of Michael.

A wave of numbing despair hit him hard. She wasn't going to fall into his arms as in all those old dreams. This was a real woman standing here, a stranger in ways all of Michael's ramblings could never have prepared him for. She was very much the Jesse he had wanted, yet more enticing, more intriguing because there were layers of her he never suspected from her husband's recollections. The truth was hard to face—that the two of them had nothing more in common than their love for the ghost who stood between them.

"It's not that I don't want to tell you, Jesse. It's just that I . . . I . . ." He stumbled to a halt, paralyzed by the sudden blaze of hope shining at him out of her eyes. "Damn, it's so hard to talk about . . . about him. Even to you. *Especially* to you."

"Try, Sloan," she urged. "Please, try. I know it has to be hard for you, remembering all of that time. I wouldn't ask it of you if there was any other way. I just can't get on with my life—not until I know."

"Okay, Jesse. I'll tell you what I can." He gave a deep sigh, relieved to face what he had to do, what he had come here to do. "You have to give me some time, though. Neither of us is in any shape to jump off this particular cliff today. Can you give me until tomorrow?"

"Of course," she agreed, though somewhat reluctantly. "We don't have to do everything all in one day. If you promise not to disappear without telling me, I can give you as long as you need."

"That's a deal." Sloan reached up and kneaded the ache at the back of his neck. "As soon as I can go out to my car without fear of drowning, I'm going back into town and get checked in at the motel. I've spent the last couple of weeks on the road with hardly any sleep. I think it's finally catching up to me."

"I could use some sleep myself. I don't think I got to bed until almost three. You wouldn't believe some of the things Bobbie told me—"

"I'm sure they were fascinating," he interrupted, clenching his teeth in disgust, "but perhaps you can tell me all about it some other time." He sincerely wished he had never heard of the guy. "We need to work out our plans for tomorrow."

Sloan didn't want to hear about her night. The dark circles beneath her eyes more than hinted at what kind of evening she'd had, and he hadn't forgotten the state of her living room when he arrived. It had definitely looked like the proverbial morning-after-the-night-before.

"How about getting me that wire hanger while I pour us a couple of glasses of orange juice? I think the rain is starting to let up."

He tried to sound more reasonable than he felt. It must have been a great job of acting. Jesse agreed and left to get the hanger. Sloan watched her go, the encouraging smile fading from his face as soon as the kitchen door closed behind her. It was a good thing the lady had no inkling of the nasty things he was wishing on her little playmate.

"Get a grip, Lassiter," he muttered. "You lived with those animals so long, you're starting to think like them. This is a civilized country. We don't do things like that out of jealousy, do we?"

"You're right, buddy," he answered softly. "We don't do them. But, by God, we still think about it."

7

MORNING DAWNED BRIGHT and glorious. The heavy
rain of the day before had washed down the dust and
filled the streams to capacity. New blades of bright
green were already sprouting among the grass that had
burned to a dry brown in the hot sun of the seemingly
endless summer.

Jesse inhaled deeply as she dug her fingers into the
wet lawn, drawing the dark and loamy incense of the
earth into her lungs, reveling in the spongy texture of
all the soil between her fingers. She was oblivious to the
mud that caked the knees of her oldest jeans and was
streaked in irregular patterns over the front of her
baggy work shirt.

She had always loved working in the yard, ever since
she was a little girl. It was the only domestic talent she
possessed, so she took great pride in preparing the
ground in the spring and cutting the grass in the summer. She especially liked getting out after a good rain
and pulling up weeds. There was something therapeu-
tic about yanking out the bunches of ragweed and
clumps of crabgrass and watching the pile of uprooted
invaders mount up as she threw them over her shoulder.

It was even more satisfying to see the grass and
blooming flowers in their beds. Her father had taught
her all she knew about gardening—it was about the
only thing they had in common. She had gotten her

looks from her mother—the curly blond hair and brown eyes were unmistakably Dorothy Green's contribution. Her father was lean and balding with hazel eyes peering out behind glasses that grew progressively thicker each year to correct his worsening nearsightedness.

Reverend Green was quiet, and serious to a fault. One day as they knelt in the yard of the parsonage, working side by side in the flower beds, Jesse had scandalized the good reverend by bragging that God might have created a whole forest, but she bet not even He could make a yard neater than theirs.

Jesse laughed aloud at the memory of her father's disapproving frown. She had felt like laughing a lot this morning. Her hangover had disappeared, receding with the passing storm. Despite all the physical trauma she had heaped on her unsuspecting body and the emotional roller-coaster ride triggered by her encounter with Sloan Lassiter, Jesse had awakened at dawn this morning in a marvelous mood.

Sloan had stayed at the house until late yesterday afternoon, waiting for the rain to stop. They had shared several pots of coffee and talked about every trivial thing they could think of to fill the silences, not mentioning again the shadowy past that awaited discussion on another day.

In the middle of the soggy afternoon, Jesse had prowled through a dozen cans of spaghetti and baked beans until she spotted a lone tin of plain chicken and had made a couple of her infamous sandwiches for their lunch. Sloan never complained and had managed to eat the whole thing without once choking on the dry bread.

When the rain had finally stopped, it was almost sundown. Jesse had followed him to the car, watching curiously as he stretched the wire hanger into an elongated double line and fashioned a curved loop at one end. He carefully eased the bent metal under the piece of rubber weather-stripping and the window glass. In less than a minute, he had slipped the wire loop over the door latch and yanked it up.

"My heavens, you're awfully good at this," she'd said with a short whistle of approval.

"Comes from being stupid enough to get myself in this kind of mess too many times." He'd looked proud of himself, despite his put-down. "I've been around too many places without locksmiths nearby. You either learn to get in on your own, or you pay for replacing a lot of smashed windows."

She'd glanced at him as he returned the hanger to nearly its original shape, straightening the metal with economical movements, smoothing out the kinks in the wire with his fingers. He had nice hands, she noticed—rectangular palms and lean, graceful fingers. There was a sprinkling of fine black hair that showed around his gold watchband where the cuffs of his shirt sleeves pulled up. She decided she liked the contrast of the dark hair against the bronzy tan of his skin.

There were a lot of things she had noticed about Sloan Lassiter. It would have been bad enough under normal circumstances to find a man so interesting, but this one was Michael's friend, here out of kindness and guilt. She stood and brushed ineffectually at the mud on her pants, trying to stop herself from thinking about the things that had plagued her most of last night.

Even after he'd gotten in his sleek car and driven away, Sloan Lassiter had never quite left her mind. There were traces of him in the house—tangible things like a second empty coffee cup instead of her solitary one, or the out-of-place dustpan he had used to sweep up the broken glass of the wine bottles. Not that he hadn't replaced everything in a neat and orderly manner—he'd left everything neater than he'd found it, but the slight difference in the way she put things away made her conscious that he'd been there.

But there were other images of Sloan that were of a more subtle and unacceptable nature—like the way he'd looked standing in the doorway when she had first seen him, drenched and dangerously familiar; the way he moved across a room with an animal kind of grace.

She frowned, annoyed that he'd made so strong an impression on her in such a short time. Not once in all the time Michael had been gone had she found herself thinking about a man—not a real, live one, she amended, dismissing her fantasy lover from the consideration. She sure had no business letting Sloan Lassiter be the first.

Even though she tried to deny his impact on her, she did allow herself to think about seeing him again tomorrow. They had to talk, she rationalized. And it was only to talk, after all. To talk about the time he had shared with Michael. Sloan was her last link with her sweet Michael—surely it was normal to want to see the man again.

Jesse felt better when she thought about Michael's presence between the two of them, insulating and protecting her even in his absence. She wasn't sure exactly why she felt the need for protection. She had moved away from her family precisely to avoid being taken care of. And Sloan had been the soul of propriety, helping her to get through a miserable day. Only once had there been any spark of danger.

She didn't think she would ever be able to forget that one endless moment on the couch when he was lying on top of her—when both of them had felt the dark and powerful stirring of something dangerous and thrillingly forbidden between them.

Between *them*, Jesse thought with a puzzled frown; between her and Sloan Lassiter, of all people. Whatever happened was a personal connection—something more than hormones—although she knew it had been too long since she had felt the weight of a man pressed against her. Jesse could tell by the glint in his eyes and the response of his body to hers that she wasn't the only one affected. Unless he looked like that at every woman he fell over. She dismissed the notion. The look on his face had been a combination of unwilling desire, embarrassment, and something else she couldn't quite pigeonhole. Jesse didn't know exactly what to call it. She had looked up into those icy blue eyes and felt . . . felt something drawing her to him—mentally as well as physically.

Yet it was the physical aspect of the attraction that concerned her most. She remembered the unmistakable solidity of his body against hers, pressing her down into the softness of the cushions, and her desire to prolong the fulfillment of her "dark stranger" fantasy.

But what was she to make of her erotic dreams about Sloan Lassiter? She chastised herself. *Remember, kid. Sloan is a real man. Your husband's friend.* So, why was she obsessive about a man she had known for only a few hours?

Why he'd probably laugh if he knew the things you've been thinking. Still are thinking.

Jesse forced herself to focus on the job at hand—gardening. Michael used to join her in the yard sometimes. He always started out helping her dig for weeds. Invariably he ended up sitting down and sifting through the damp soil with his fingers, examining every pebble to make sure it wasn't a chip of pottery or a shard of bone.

"Look, Jesse," he would say. "Come see what I've found."

"Get back to work, slacker. This isn't an archaeological dig, you know."

Nevertheless, she would always put down whatever she was doing and come to sit beside him in the sunshine. It was fun listening to him.

"This is a piece of Indian pottery, honey." He held a mud-colored bit of rock with exquisite carefulness. "Can you even imagine how long this has been here in the ground? In our yard, under this flower bed?"

"Thousands of years?" she asked, smiling as he scarcely glanced up at her, so intently was he studying the fragment.

"Thousands of years," he began. "You can tell by the glaze used on the surface. And look... There are distinctive markings that identify it as—"

"Earth to Michael Varner," Jesse interrupted, leaning over to whisper in his ear. "Come in, Professor Varner."

Michael looked up at her and grinned. With a shrug of apology, he slipped the piece of pottery into his front shirt pocket for safekeeping.

"Sorry, Jesse. I get carried away sometimes."

"Really? I hadn't noticed."

What was with her today? Either she was fantasizing about the future with Sloan or she was back in the past with Michael. She grabbed a shovel and began furiously digging out the weeds in the flower bed.

"YOU'RE A REAL IDIOT, Lassiter," he mumbled to himself. "It takes someone seven kinds of stupid to still be hanging around this town, much less meeting the woman for dinner."

He looked around the room, more to kill time than out of any real interest in the decor. Not too bad as Mexican restaurants went. At least it didn't have murals of quaint villages painted on every available surface. The rosy pink adobe walls were hung with *ristras* of chilis and strings of garlic. Deep earth shades of terracotta tiles warmed the floors. Best of all, there wasn't a painting of a bullfighter on black velvet to be seen.

"One point for you, Ms. Varner," he said, trying to remember not to talk aloud. "Careful, J. Sloan. With this many people in the room, one of them might be a shrink, and you don't want to talk to any more of those guys for a while, do you?"

Sloan sampled a couple of the crispy fried tortilla pieces dunked in the highly seasoned tomato, onion and red chili salsa that the waitress had brought with his drink. The salsa was hot enough to bring tears to his eyes—just the way he liked it—but he found he wasn't in the mood for food.

He wished for the tenth time that Jesse Varner had chosen another restaurant for their meeting. Any other restaurant would have been fine. Surely there had to be someplace more suitable for a serious conversation than Rosa's Hacienda.

The place was a zoo, for Pete's sake—a classy, trendy sort of zoo. If Jesse ever got here, they would have more peace and quiet at a table for two in the middle of Grand Central Station. Almost every one of the varnished white pine tables was occupied by two or more well-dressed diners. And they all seemed intent on talking at the top of their lungs or laughing boisterously.

Sloan felt conspicuously alone in the midst of so much easy friendliness. He glanced accusingly at the empty chair across from him.

He fidgeted and hoped the waitress would come by again to see if he wanted anything. For the last half hour she had been virtually his shadow. Now that he was ready for another drink, she seemed to have disappeared from the face of the earth.

He turned slightly in his chair, craning his neck around to try to find her. Instead, he was facing the doorway as Jesse walked in. The sight of her almost made him fall out of his chair.

"Lordy mercy," he whispered in awed tones. "This was definitely worth waiting for."

Even the morning after an all-night bender, she had been something to see, but Jesse Varner dressed for a night out was truly a sight to behold. He watched her as she walked across the room toward him, praying the expression on his face wasn't as openly lustful as those of the other men staring at her. He didn't blame them; he just didn't want to get caught in the act.

Jesse wasn't a flashy dresser. With her looks, she didn't need to be. Sloan had no doubt Miss Manners herself would have approved wholeheartedly of the off-white linen skirt and jacket, and matching mid-heeled shoes. The only touches of color were a burnt-orange blouse and small button earrings of the same shade.

Then again, if old Emily had seen things from his point of view, she would have had to rethink her whole theory of proper attire. Looking at Jesse Varner gave him ideas that were not only improper; they were downright embarrassing.

He could only think of how the straight skirt emphasized the narrowness of her waist and the length of her gorgeous legs. "Legs that went all the way up to there," as the old saying went. There was something about the way the light reflected off the silky fabric of her blouse that made him want to offer to help her off with her jacket.

And, although she was almost as tall as he was, he really liked seeing her in those shoes. Nothing looked sexier than a tall, beautiful woman in a pair of heels. She lifted one hand and pushed back a strand of hair, and he amended that: nothing looked sexier than a tall, beautiful *blonde* in a pair of heels.

She walked with all the natural grace and poise of a fashion model coming down a runway—head back, eyes focused straight ahead, seemingly blind to all the attention she was attracting. A couple sitting at a table just inside the room called her name, and Jesse stopped to speak to them briefly.

To his astonishment, Sloan was more impressed with her each time he saw her. All day long, he'd been trying to convince himself that Jesse wasn't quite as great looking as he'd thought when he first saw her yesterday morning. Wrong. Wrong. Wrong.

It was becoming hard to deny that the woman was getting to him in a serious way.

Besides the fact that she was beautiful or that he had become obsessed with thinking about her during his imprisonment, there was something in her spirit—an honesty and lack of pretense—that was rare enough to be remarkable. Hell, was she ever honest! Even when it didn't cast her in a particularly rosy light.

Take her little night of overindulgence, for instance. Instead of coming up with excuses for herself and laying the blame on her boyfriend, Jesse had taken total responsibility for her own actions. She hadn't pretended to be an innocent victim, nor had she said one bad word about how the guy had left her to fend for herself without even calling the next day to check on her.

Sloan didn't think much of her friend Bobby, but then again, he wasn't inclined to look favorably on any man she was involved with. Not that it was any of his business who she was dating. He hadn't expected her to wear widow's weeds and join a nunnery after Michael's death, but—

He shook his head, trying to stop the images of Jesse being pursued by another man—by other men. It didn't matter who they were, even if most of them were bound to be more considerate than her friend Bobby. It rankled to think about that guy. Jesse was so beautiful— far too beautiful to put up with being treated so casually. And she didn't even seem to notice that she deserved better.

Sloan sighed, unable to escape his memories of the long hours he and Michael had spent talking about their lives. He dreaded having to dredge up all the old pain, but that was what this meeting was about. Jesse wanted to hear about her husband, and there was no one else who could answer her questions.

Damn. Why did he have to do this? Only a fool would feel this much loyalty to a dead man—especially to a dead man who had a wife like Jesse.

Jesse was nearly to the table when she finally spotted him in the crowd and made eye contact. The effect was instantaneous, like being hit in the back of the head with a velvet hammer. She smiled at him and he felt it in his bones.

"Have you been waiting long?"

He stood to pull out her chair.

"No, I just got here myself," he lied. "Let me get the waitress to bring you a drink."

He stood behind her chair and pushed it in for her, inhaling her perfume. His fingers rested only a fraction of an inch from the place where her hair hung down over the wooden slats of the back of the chair.

All I need to do is lift my hand a couple of inches. She'd never notice if I did it. Just a touch. He lifted his hand and brought it a millimeter closer to temptation. Then, with a motion so gentle it barely existed, he brushed the backs of his fingers against the soft, tangled curls.

"Please, don't." Jesse turned and looked up at him, a slight frown shadowing her gold-brown eyes. "Don't do that."

"I'm sorry." Sloan jerked his hand back and looked down at her, hating himself for making her look so uncomfortable. He hesitated, trying to frame an apology for his breach of manners. "I didn't mean to offend you. I just—"

"You don't need to apologize," she said, brushing aside his explanation. "And you don't need to be in such a rush to get me a drink. I won't get the shakes without one, you know."

"A drink?" Relief flooded through him, replacing the self-disgust he felt at being caught fondling her hair. "I didn't mean to give that impression, Jesse. I just thought you might want to have something from the bar."

"Be honest. You assumed after yesterday that I couldn't get through the meal without a drink."

"And why would I assume any such thing?"

"You don't have to be so polite." Jesse glanced up at him, unable to hide the flush of embarrassment that stained her cheeks. "I know you think I'm a total lush. After the condition you found me in when you arrived, how could you help it?"

"That isn't what I was thinking at all," Sloan answered honestly. He was sorry to see her being so hard on herself. "Don't make such a big deal out of a simple question."

"You're right. I guess I was being too defensive." She hitched her chair a little closer to the table and motioned for him to sit down. "I just don't want you to think I make a habit of drinking so much. To tell the truth, I hardly ever drink at all. That's probably why it hit me so hard."

"Four bottles of wine would hit most people pretty hard, Jesse."

As soon as the words were out, he regretted saying them. Her chin came up and she stared defiantly across the table at him. *Smart move, Lassiter. Why don't you throw a little more gasoline on the fire? You'd better cool it, or she's going to be out of here like a shot.*

"I told you I didn't drink it all by myself. Not that it's really any of your business."

"You're right about that." Sloan tried to phrase a neutral reply, hoping to defuse her defensive attitude. "It's none of my business how much you drink or with whom."

"I appreciate all you did to help me, but it doesn't give you the right to sit there and lecture me about my private life."

"Well, excuse me for overstepping my bounds." His temper reached the limits of its flexibility and snapped back into action. "Evidently, all I'm supposed to do is show up and clean up the mess some other guy is making of your life."

"What's that supposed to mean?" she demanded indignantly. "What other guy are you talking about?"

"Was he so unimpressive you forgot his name, or are you going to blame your memory lapse on the booze, too?"

Sloan knew before she answered that he'd pushed her too far. He didn't for the life of him know why he was acting like such a bastard, giving her the third degree about her personal life. It was as if he wanted to make her mad, to push her so far that she would get up and leave. He glanced at her hands resting on the table in tight-fisted balls and realized she was very close to losing her temper and walking out.

"After the way we met, I can understand that you might have gotten the wrong impression of me." She spoke quietly, but her teeth were clenched so tightly the words came out in a half-articulated hiss. "And, taking that into consideration, I'm trying hard not to be insulted, but I don't think you have any right to talk to me this way."

"Ah, hell, I know it," he admitted, regretting that he hadn't kept his mouth shut. "I'm sorry. I don't know you well enough to be jumping to that kind of conclusion."

"You don't really know me at all, Mr. Lassiter. Until yesterday—"

"What happened to calling me *Sloan?*" he interrupted. "I thought we were going to be on friendly, first-name terms."

"What happened to treating me like a friend?" Jesse didn't back down an inch, holding his gaze with her intense brown eyes. "If we aren't going to be able to get along with each other, I don't see any reason to bother with this meeting at all."

"I thought you wanted to talk about Michael."

"I want to hear about that more than anything, but not if it means you and I have to tear at each other all evening." Her voice was ragged, revealing how stressed she was. "Michael would have hated this. Maybe I'd better leave."

When she started to stand, he reached out and took her hand. Sloan hated himself for being such an obstinate bully. He had come more than a thousand miles to talk to this woman. Damned if he was going to blow it because of a fit of jealousy.

"Don't go, Jess. I think we ought to just sit down and have our dinner. Then we can relax for a while, and start this whole conversation over again on a more friendly basis." Sloan glossed over their discord and looked around for the waitress. "Sound like a good idea?"

"I'd like that, but I don't know if it's going to be possible."

Jesse was looking at him with an expression he found hard to figure out. Her skin was pale as a ghost, and there was fear in her eyes.

"Do you mind telling me why not?"

"I don't know if I can," she said, shaking her head uncertainly. "At least not without sounding melodramatic or mystical or something." She paused as if waiting for him to comment, then took a deep breath and continued. "There's something going on here . . . something about you that I don't understand. It frightens me a little."

"You're afraid of me?"

Sloan didn't like that notion at all. In fact, seeing her sitting there, looking at him with such unrelenting suspicion, made him unaccountably miserable. He hadn't come here to hurt her or to frighten her. Hell, if he was going to make her feel so badly, he ought to leave right now, before things got any worse.

"It's not just you I'm afraid of, Sloan." Jesse reached her hand out toward him, then obviously thought better of the gesture and withdrew it. "There's just something between you and me that I don't understand. You ought to be a stranger to me, but sometimes I get these flashes of having seen you before, in circumstances I know aren't real." Her voice dropped to a husky whisper. "Dreams... I have the strangest dreams sometimes...."

She hesitated, studying her own fingers with concentration. Sloan wanted to hear more. He was oddly thrilled by her confession. The idea that she thought of him was fodder for his own fantasies, though he didn't like it that her thoughts were so disturbing to her.

"I think it's only normal for you to respond to me on a subconscious level, Jesse. And since my name has been linked in your mind with all the bad things that happened to Michael, it's only natural for you to feel a little threatened by me."

He hated what he was saying, wanted to beg her not to believe it, but instead he went on, trying to soothe her fears with the psychobabble the shrinks had tried on him for weeks on end.

"Just let it out, honey. I promise it won't kill me if you need to work out some of your anger on me. Michael's gone and I'm the one most closely linked to him, both in the media and in your mind. You can tell me about it if you want to. I'll try to understand." He forced a laugh, knowing it sounded as painful as it felt. "I understand bad dreams better than most people, believe me."

"I can understand the bad dreams," she said, glancing up at him for a moment before lowering her eyes in what looked like embarrassment. "I've learned to live with nightmares. I know what those dreams mean. But . . ."

"Go on, Jess," he urged. "You can tell me about it."

"The dreams aren't always nightmares, exactly."

"Do you want to talk about your dreams, Jesse? Sometimes it helps to have someone besides yourself to talk to."

"Sometimes talking only stirs up more problems."

She sounded more frightened than before when she said that, and his heart went out to her. He was overcome by a wave of tenderness and protectiveness that made him want to hold her tightly against him so that he could absorb all the pain.

She straightened in her chair and squared her shoulders as if facing up to the unspoken surge of longing he couldn't contain.

"There's not much to tell. Really, Sloan. Just crazy stuff. Things that don't make any sense."

She glanced up at him, studying him for a few seconds with a strangely intent expression before looking back down at her hands. She twisted her wedding ring absently, focusing his attention on the simple band of gold that bound her still to her late husband. To Michael.

He suddenly remembered the reason he had come here in the first place. Michael—Michael as he had last seen him, thin and ill, shivering with the fever that claimed him only hours later. The young man had only one thought as he faced the certainty of his death, one request.

And now, it's time for me to make good on my promise, Michael. I'm not going to let my feelings for Jesse stop me. I just hope the most dangerous thing I have to protect her from isn't myself.

"Don't be afraid to talk to me, Jesse," he said, breaking the silence between them. "Whatever we have to face, we can get through it. I'm not the kind of man who has a lot of faith in things I can't see, but I think you may be right about you and me. There are things happening here—and they may be things neither of us may understand—but I don't think either of us can get on with our lives until we get them settled."

"Things about Michael?"

"Yeah, that's a big part of it."

"But it's not all of it, is it?"

"I don't think so, Jess." He couldn't hide the uncertainty he was feeling. "But I think we need to take it slow right now. Give ourselves a little time to get to know each other before we get too deep into trying to figure it all out."

"Do we have any time, Sloan?" she asked. "You keep talking about getting to know each other, but when is that going to happen? Does that mean you're planning to stay here in Taos for a while?"

"I'll be around, at least for a few weeks. I haven't decided exactly what I want to work at right now. There are several companies I want to talk to before I decide."

"Here in Taos?" She appeared skeptical. "I don't think you'll find much opportunity for a high-powered executive in this little town, and somehow I don't see you giving ski lessons or working in a sporting-goods store."

"Come on, now. Don't you think I could sell hip boots and fishing lures to the tourists?"

"Do you know much about fishing?"

"I can tell the difference between a trout and a worm," he bragged, laughing aloud at her theatrical groan of dismay. "And, just for backup purposes, I have interviews with a couple of companies in Denver and a good job offer in Albuquerque. Maybe if the fishing business is in a slump these days, I shouldn't cancel those right away?"

"Maybe not," she said with a smile. "What kind of jobs are you considering?"

"Why don't we discuss it over an order of nachos? All this serious talk about work and life makes me hungry." She agreed and he sighed in relief, finally catching sight of the waitress. "Heaven is on our side. The vanishing lady has returned."

The harried-looking young woman, balancing a tray of drinks and chips, was trapped between two tables, obviously trying her best not to scream in frustration at her demanding customers. When the party of four in front of her finally got settled at a table, clearing her path, she nodded at Sloan to show that she hadn't forgotten him and would be right back to take their order.

As she moved on to deliver the drinks, the couple just behind her called out to Jesse and waved. She looked up curiously, then waved back. Sloan knew by her friendly expression what she wanted even before she asked him. He didn't really share her enthusiasm at having to meet new people, especially right now, before he and Jesse had a chance to feel comfortable with each other.

"Those are two of my favorite people, Sloan. Would you mind if I invite them over for a drink? I'd really like for you to meet them."

It was plain from her uncertain tone that she really cared whether or not he minded. His reservations melted away in the warmth of her sensitivity to his feelings. Hell, when she looked at him like that, as if what he wanted mattered so much to her, she could invite everyone in Taos over for drinks, and he'd smile when he picked up the tab.

"Sure, Jesse. I'd like to meet your friends."

"Are you sure you don't mind?"

"Of course not." He forced a casual reply, hoping he sounded more relaxed than he felt. Wanting to emphasize his full cooperation, he added, "Since we haven't ordered, would you like to ask them to join us for dinner?"

"What a great idea!" Her glow of pleasure was worth the sacrifice of their privacy. "Let me go and ask them before they get settled in over there."

She stood and smoothed her skirt, drawing his attention once again to the alluring swell of her hips beneath the fabric. It took all the willpower he could muster not to look too long, not to let her see how affected he was by the way she moved.

"I wouldn't have gotten through the last year without these guys. I know you're going to like them both, especially Bobbie."

He nodded vaguely, having lost track of the conversation for a split second, catching the last thing she said after she had turned and walked away. Suddenly her parting sentence caught up with him, freezing the forced smile on his lips, turning his face into the mask of a gargoyle.

"Especially Bobby." Oh, he'd heard her words, all right. It just took an extra couple of seconds for them to sink in.

"Bobby?" he said, coming back to earth with a thud.

"Bobby?" he repeated louder, with a much less pleasant inflection. "Face facts, old boy. You're about to have dinner with good old Bobby, Jesse's favorite drinking buddy."

8

SLOAN WATCHED THE tableau unfolding before him, staring in disbelief. At first glance, Bobby was less than impressive. He was perhaps a couple of inches over six feet tall, definitely on the skinny side, and his hair was a nondescript shade of brownish blond.

"How does this guy do it? He looks more like Clark Kent than Casanova, but he's surrounded by two women, and they're both putty in his hands."

Sloan continued to stare as Jesse greeted the couple. When she reached up to kiss Bobby on the cheek, neither the man nor she seemed to be the slightest bit ill at ease, nor did the other woman's friendly smile so much as waver.

Something was screwy here. How could a nebbish like Bobby end up with the two best-looking women in town? And without having to sneak around to avoid being killed by one of them? It just didn't figure. Sloan looked from one woman to the other, then back again, his mind still not coming up with a logical reason why either of these women would accept such a shabby situation.

The petite brunette at Bobby's side was quite an eye-catcher in her own right. She was tiny—maybe five-feet-two if you didn't subtract the strappy high-heeled sandals she wore—yet she managed to pack a lot of appeal into every inch. Her chocolate-brown hair was short and shiny with wispy bangs that brought to mind the gamine quality of a young Audrey Hepburn. The wide, white-toothed smile she flashed as Jesse approached was genuine and unmistakably welcoming.

Sloan glanced at Bobby's face, expecting at least a trace of unease as the women in his life came face-to-face. But Bobby was as cool as ice. He just stood there looking perfectly content, smiling as the two women hugged each other, looking for all the world like bosom buddies.

Sloan shook his head in wonder. You had to hand it to the guy, even if he was a slimy bastard—he had them both eating out of his hand. Whatever he was doing, it was obviously working.

Then, as if on cue, Jesse, Bobby, and the dark-haired gamine turned to look in his direction. Sloan nodded at Jesse, wishing he knew what the hell she was telling them about him. The expressions on their faces were curious, but not unfriendly, as they looked for him, politely eager to size him up.

Then they picked him out of the crowd, and Sloan saw the faint but unmistakable air of concern dampen their welcoming smiles as they realized that Jesse was in the company of such a dark and hard-faced man as he appeared to be. He recognized their apprehension and wished, not for the first time, that he had one of those easy faces—the facile smile and a touch of boyish charm—that put people immediately at ease. It would sure be an advantage tonight to be able to start out with that kind of edge.

He took a deep breath as the three friends approached the table, not knowing why he was so nervous. It wasn't that big a deal whether they liked him or not. He had to look after Jesse, both as a matter of honor and because he wanted to, but nothing said he had to be best pals with all her boyfriends.

"Sloan, I'd like you to meet two people who have kept me going these last few months."

Sloan held out his hand in greeting. The hand that gripped his in return was strong and warmly enfolding. As he met the man's direct, gray eyes, he found curiosity, but no apparent hostility. There wasn't an inkling of rivalry, but rather what looked amazingly like an admiring glint of respect in the man's eyes.

What the hell is with this guy? Sloan thought. He should at the very least be checking me out as competition, not looking at me as if he was thinking of buying me a beer. And there were Jesse and the brunette standing beside each other, happy as two long-lost sisters. Damn, but this was a strange little group!

"Nice to meet you, Bobby," he said coolly. "Jesse has mentioned your name several times, but I never thought I'd be running into you like this."

"I guess she didn't fill you in on many details about me, did she?"

An amused and distinctly female voice came from the woman at Jesse's side, a voice that held more than a touch of laughter. Sloan turned to face her, dropping the man's hand like a hot potato. The petite woman gave him a wink, then held out her hand toward him.

"*I'm* Bobbie. Bobbie Stone." Her laughter bubbled out, but the warm light in her eyes took away any hint of malice. "This is my husband, Hank."

"Bobbie." Sloan glanced back at the man he'd just shaken hands with, then turned his attention to the woman who was holding his hand in both of hers. "Hello, Bobbie. And Hank. Pleased to meet you both."

"And a little surprised, obviously," Bobbie said, not bothering to try to hide her delight at being the victim of mistaken identity. "No need to apologize. Happens all the time."

As they pulled out chairs and sat down, Sloan managed to catch Jesse's attention, letting her know with a lift of his eyebrows and a stern shake of his head that her demure expression didn't fool him for a minute. She had known all along that he assumed Bobbie was Bobby. It didn't take a rocket scientist to figure out that she had let him leap to all sorts of conclusions while she sat back and let him make noises like a judgmental prig.

"I'm afraid Sloan met me the morning after our last little evening together and assumed you were one of my rowdy gentlemen callers," Jesse said with an unrepentant smirk, letting him know she was less than impressed with his glowering. "He was having so much fun disapproving of the relationship that I couldn't spoil it by confessing that you were a rather respectable mother of two Boy Scouts."

"You use the term *respectable* a little more loosely than some people in this town, Jesse." Hank kept his voice low and slid a glance around to see if anyone was listening to them. "I wish you two girls took life a bit more seriously."

"My gosh, Hank, lighten up. You take life seriously enough for all of us." Bobbie interrupted her husband's grave warning with a wave of her hand. "We sat in the privacy of Jesse's living room and drank a little too much. I don't think that's grounds for being run out of town for corrupting the public morals."

"People do talk," Hank said direly. "In our position—"

"Oh, not here, honey," Bobbie groaned. "I thought we were going to go out and have a good time and forget about work."

"Hank is the principal of the school where I work," Jesse explained. "He doesn't have a very high opinion of teachers who lead his wife into corruption."

"And Lord knows, I fought you all the way." Bobbie struck a prim pose for a moment, not succeeding terribly well in her role.

Hank rolled his eyes heavenward, muttering faintly under his breath. Jesse and Bobbie dissolved into laughter, making no attempt to hide their giggles or their teasing. Hank just sat there and stared at them, looking so very much like a stern principal that Sloan smiled in spite of himself.

As they talked Sloan relaxed, pleased more than he could have imagined to meet Bobbie. The light was beginning to dawn as he remembered Michael's talking about his old friend Hank and his wife. But that wasn't what Michael called her. Not Bobbie, he mused. Roberta? No. It was Berta. He was sure of it. Finding an answer put him a little more at ease, and he tuned back in to the conversation as Jesse finished the story.

"If we weren't all such old friends, I'm pretty sure he would have asked the school board to replace me." It was plain from her tone that Jesse didn't believe a word of it. She reached over and patted Hank's arm, and the tightness around his mouth eased a little. "Hank is one of those rare individuals who likes living life in the safe middle of the road. He doesn't understand why some people get a little crazy from time to time."

"I'm sure we all need to let our hair down sometime." Sloan looked at Hank, then back at Jesse. "Even those of us who have a reputation to look after."

"Hank looks after all of our reputations. He always has, even when we were all just kids." Jesse smiled fondly and her friends responded, looking at each other with the love and easy familiarity forged over years. "We all grew up together, you know. Whenever we got ourselves into some kind of scrape, Hank figured out a way to justify it."

"More often than not, I ended up being the scapegoat." Hank sounded dour, but the twinkle in his eyes ruined the effect. "None of you guys ever took a minute to stop and consider the long-range consequences of those stunts you pulled."

"That wasn't our job, honey," Bobbie said with a fond smile of remembrance. "We had our hands full coming up with things to do." She made an effort to include Sloan in their trip down memory lane. "Michael was the idea man. I was props."

"I got to be the mouthpiece." Jesse turned in her chair to face him more directly. "Being the minister's daughter had its advantages sometimes. Everyone believed me, so when we got into one of our scrapes, I took over. When I looked really angelic and explained how we got involved in something, we usually managed to squeak our way out of trouble."

She opened her brown eyes wide and assumed an expression of such sweet innocence it made Sloan's heart pound. Anyone with a face like that could get away with murder. She held him mesmerized for a few seconds before winking and spoiling the effect. He suspected she didn't realize the slow, deliberate wink was just as devastating as the practiced innocence.

"And Hank was the group conscience, right?" Sloan recalled how Michael's eyes had twinkled as he described the long lectures Hank had subjected them to. "The lifetime president of Guilt, Incorporated."

The other three turned as one and stared at him. He didn't realize until he saw the shock in their eyes and the wave of paleness cross Jesse's face the impact his words would have. Bobbie recovered her voice first.

"You and Michael must have scraped the bottom of the barrel for you to have known about that," she said, serious for the first time he'd seen her. "My God, you two must have gotten close to share such little details."

"Yeah, I guess we did. After eighteen months together, there aren't many things that don't get said."

Sloan looked around for the waitress, trying to see anything except the shadow of pain in Jesse's eyes. Hank and Bobbie watched him expectantly, obviously waiting for him to tell them more. He gave up on ordering another drink and wished to hell he could get away from the gentle grilling he sensed was about to begin. God, he didn't want to go over all that again, not even for Jesse. They were asking too much. Maybe it would be easier to just tell them how hard it was.

That urge died even as it was born. These people loved Michael. They didn't need to hear about the long months of despair, the agonizing nights when both men had given up hope of ever leaving or seeing their homes or loved ones again. Michael's loved ones. Sloan looked at their faces and knew he couldn't tell them that, no matter how bitter he felt. He searched for a way to explain it without hurting them too much, but he couldn't quite keep the anger and pain from his voice.

"We talked and talked and then we went over everything again. It beat listening to the walls close in. No television. No radio. No quick little jaunts to trendy restaurants to chat for hours with our friends."

Nobody filled the uncomfortable silence when he stopped talking for a few seconds, but he felt their encouragement and sympathetic stares. It irritated him even further to be the focus of their pity. Especially Jesse's. The last thing he wanted from her was pity. He clamped down hard on that thought, not wanting to give his mind a chance to tell him what he did want from her. This night was rough enough without having to fight those particular monsters. Back to the unpleasant task at hand.

"Mostly Michael talked and I listened. He had a way of making even the most mundane things sound like high adventure. All those stories about his family..." Sloan looked up at Jesse and found her watching him. He let himself be soothed for a moment by the warmth in her eyes before he continued. "I don't think he ever knew how much those stories meant to me—how much I got from what he called his 'endless prattle.'"

Sloan swallowed hard, trying not to let himself get caught up in the emotions of remembrance. This wasn't going at all well. There was too much pain welling up to be talking. He swallowed again and wished to hell he had never started the story. The long stretch of awkward silence was broken by Hank.

"Michael enjoyed talking to people, *needed* to be able to talk." Hank spoke with a quiet calmness, but the mask of his glasses didn't hide the sadness in his eyes. "He was lucky to have a friend like you there to share things with."

"Luck of the draw," Sloan said with as much coolness as he could manage. "He probably would have been better off with a cell mate who did more than listen. I'm not the most forthcoming conversationalist in the world."

"Sometimes listening is the most important part of talking," Hank said. "You were there for him."

"I was there, period. I didn't have any more choice in the matter than he did."

"All the same, you and he became friends. I can hear it in your voice, Sloan. I'm glad he had you."

"It was no big deal. Anyone can listen. Michael would have gotten along with anyone in the same situation. He—"

"Don't kid yourself, Sloan," Jesse interrupted, pulling his attention back to her, despite his efforts to the contrary. "Michael did love to talk, but he wasn't in the habit of really opening himself up to just anyone. Hank and Bobbie, myself, maybe a few others were let in. Some of the things he shared with you prove he came to trust you a great deal."

"Maybe that was his biggest mistake. Maybe that's why he's dead."

"No, Sloan. Don't say things like that." Jesse reached over and touched the back of his hand where it lay clenched into a white-knuckled fist on the table. "You aren't to blame."

Sloan jerked his hand away from hers, unable to bear the gentle touch of her fingers. His reaction was too abrupt to be subtle and he saw the look Hank and Bobbie exchanged before they both glanced discreetly away. He hated causing a scene, but he had only minimal control over the situation. It was important to settle all this, once and for all. There was no way he could sit here and handle a long, drawn-out postmortem. This was turning into a morbid little wake, and he didn't have the inclination to bare his soul, especially in front of this couple he barely knew.

"Face it, Jess. If he hadn't run into me, maybe he would never have been in that stinking place at all. If it hadn't been for me, Michael would be alive right now." Sloan stood and pushed back his chair. "I'm not some kind of hero, people. I'm just a survivor." He took a couple of bills from his wallet and put them on the table. "I'm sorry if I've spoiled everyone's dinner, but this isn't going to work."

"Sloan. Don't go." Jesse gestured to his empty chair, an imploring light in her dark eyes. "Sit down and eat, please. We don't have to talk about—"

"Maybe Bobbie and I should go and let the two of you talk." Hank started to get to his feet, but Sloan shook his head and motioned for them to stay.

"No, you guys go ahead." Good manners took over and he made an attempt to soften the bluntness of his words and impulsive departure. "It was good to meet both of you. Maybe we can get together for a talk before I leave town."

"Leave?" Jesse asked in a tight voice. "But last night you said—"

"I'm sorry, Jess," he said, noticing that Hank and Bobbie were still looking on with curious, if friendly, interest. Sloan wished again that he could be charming instead of blunt and graceless, but right at the moment he didn't have the strength to deal with social niceties. "I just can't handle this right now."

"Please, Sloan. Sit down and talk." Jesse hesitated, then corrected herself. "No, we don't have to talk. We can eat. Just don't go."

"I am sorry, but . . . ." He hated making her unhappy, but this wasn't going to get any better. "Sorry."

There was a shocked silence as he stood over them. Bobbie looked up at him, all the pert animation wiped from her face as Hank's expression became even more sober.

But all that really mattered was Jesse. Sloan expected some response, some outburst of blame or denial, but there was nothing—nothing that he could read. She didn't even blink as he looked down at her, and her eyes were focused on some faraway place that only she could see. She was frozen there, as lovely and waxen as a mannequin—and as unreachable.

Sloan muttered another apology and turned away, wishing again that he was anyplace on earth except here. He turned and made his way across the room and out to the parking lot. By the time he got to his car his hands were shaking and his legs felt as though they were made of rubber. Instead of unlocking the door and getting in, he slumped against the car, bracing his hands on the top and laying his head against the cool metal, trying to reorient himself.

He arched his back, stretching like a cat, in an effort to work out the hard knots of tension in the muscles between his shoulder blades. Maybe this was so hard because he wasn't cut out for all this nice-guy stuff. It would be smarter and a hell of a lot easier to get out of here while he still could, just to forget all his promises to Michael to take care of Jesse.

In the first place, the only person he'd made any deals with was dead and gone; and after all, Jesse had friends to look out for her. Hank and Berta—Bobbie—would do a better job of it than he could, any day of the week. Yeah, he thought, pouring salve on his conscience. As soon as he could get himself together, he was going to do her a favor and get out of here. "What a piece of work you are, J. Sloan," he muttered. "What a spineless bastard you turned out to be."

He heard the staccato click of heels on concrete—high heels, coming up fast behind him. Jesse. The now familiar blend of sandalwood and amber, borne by a faint breeze, announced her presence. He breathed a word of thanks that he had even a fraction of a second's warning, a moment in which to steel his expression before he faced her.

"I'm sorry about the scene, Jesse." The words were properly apologetic, but he made no effort to sound overtly solicitous. "I know you want some details, some nice stories to hold on to, but I can't bury myself in the past anymore. And you shouldn't, either, if you want my advice."

"I've heard just about all the advice I can stand for a while, Sloan," she said, looking at him with surprisingly calm brown eyes. "I don't mean to be ghoulish or dwell on all that time you need to forget. That's not it at all, really." She stepped closer to where he stood by the car and ran the fingers of one hand idly over the shiny strip of chrome on the fender. "It's all tied up with Michael, but it's not only that. I want to get to know you."

"Come on, Jess. You want to wring me out and save all the bits of your husband I can give you."

"That's not true. Not the way you say it."

"Say it however you want to, baby. Whatever makes you feel less guilty. Just don't waste all that soft soap trying to pump me about him. Pretending to like me to dig it all up is going pretty far."

"That's an ugly thing to imply."

"It's an ugly thing to do, Jesse," he replied with cold fury. "You and I had better walk away from each other now. If we don't, I have a feeling things might get a lot worse before they get better."

She flinched slightly at his angry response, but he was fighting hard for the strength to walk away. If he gave in to the urge to comfort her, there would be more complications than either of them was prepared to deal with.

"You promised you were going to stay for a while," she reminded, looking at him and lifting her chin as if to dare him to argue the point. "You said we'd have time to—"

"Aren't you listening to anything I've said, Jesse? This isn't a church picnic. There are things going on that neither of us is in control of, lady. If I stayed around here—"

He caught himself before the threat became verbal, but there was a leap of blue flame in his eyes as they skimmed up and down her body. There was an answering flicker of awareness in her own eyes and she didn't blink or look away.

"I'm not afraid."

"You should be, Jess. We both should be."

"Just don't run away, Sloan."

The wind blew a stream of blond hair across her face, masking her mouth and making her eyes glow darker and more dangerously than ever. Impatiently she tossed back the thick mass and continued, not noticing how fascinated he was by her action.

"Give us a chance to get to know each other. If all we have in common is Michael, then at least we'll find that out. Will you try?"

"I don't think—"

"You've had too much thinking time for too long. That's part of the problem." Jesse was serious, and she studied his face carefully for a few seconds before she added quietly, "Stay and give yourself a chance to see what you want, not what you *think* you should want. Stay. For a few days, at least. Stay."

Sloan fought to keep from reaching out to pull her against him and demonstrate exactly what he wanted— what he had wanted for so long—but he didn't trust himself to be able to deal with his own warning. Both of them were emotionally fragile right now, and he knew better what was simmering below the surface than she did. He looked into her face and saw the shadow of need and longing that he knew all too well. He also knew he wasn't going anywhere until this was settled, one way or another.

9

JESSE LOOKED DOWN AT her wristwatch and scolded herself for being late. There didn't seem to be enough hours in the days anymore. Since J. Sloan Lassiter first showed up at her door, time seemed to have slipped off its well-worn schedule. Five weeks had gone by so quickly she could hardly believe it.

Sloan had been around Taos most weekends. Much to her surprise, he was checking out jobs in New Mexico and Colorado. He liked the peace and quiet of the mountains, or so he said. She liked to think maybe he liked being close to her enough for that to influence his decision about where to settle. There had been lots of offers from all over the country. Sloan was unimpressed, dismissing most of them as "jackals trying to capitalize on yesterday's news."

Jesse didn't care what their motives were; she just hoped one of the "jackals" who lived nearby would come up with an offer good enough to keep Sloan close enough that they could stay in touch. She was still mulling over the possibilities as she pulled off the highway onto the short road leading to her house.

The first thing she saw was Sloan's Maserati parked in the driveway. The sight of it made her spirits soar.

He's here. She almost sang the words aloud. *He's finally here.*

She had been expecting him—his last letter had said he would be back this weekend—but until she saw the car she hadn't realized how much she was looking forward to his arrival, or just how badly she had missed him.

Sloan's first visit had stretched into ten days, some of which had been more awkward than enjoyable. By mutual consent they had tried not to talk about Michael all the time, even though it often ended up that way. It was too easy to let every evening turn into a melancholy exchange of remembrances, but gradually they'd discovered things they had in common—things that Michael wasn't a direct part of.

Jesse had played tour guide while Sloan performed the duties of a driver. She loved sitting in the passenger seat of the sports car, watching the scenery flash by as she filled him in on a bit of history or pointed out an unusual rock formation. It also gave her an opportunity, from behind the protective barrier of her sunglasses, to observe Sloan without being caught staring.

And she did enjoy watching him. He handled the powerful car with exquisite nonchalance. He didn't try to fill every silence with empty chatter, but he was by no means a poor conversationalist. He seemed to be greatly amused by her enthusiastic questions.

Jesse had been amazed that he wanted to hear about her life, especially the past three years. It was quite an ego boost to see a glint of respect in his eyes as she told him about her job and "her kids" at school. The only time they ran into trouble was when they discussed Michael. Those conversations invariably led to Sloan getting stonily quiet and gripping the steering wheel until she thought he would break it or his fingers. Jesse had gradually learned not to start every sentence with "Michael always . . ."

After Jesse had showed Sloan all the sights Taos had to offer, they'd branched out from there. They'd made several day trips—checking out the Puye Indian cliff dwellings near Santa Clara and browsing through the art galleries and Governor's Palace in Santa Fe. When school began, she'd been disappointed to have to restrict their traveling to weekends.

Sloan had fallen into the habit of dropping her a little note or postcard every day he was away, letting her know about his progress. It had been almost three weeks since his last visit, and Jesse could hardly bear waiting another minute. The wheels of her car had scarcely stopped rolling before she jumped out and bounded up the steps of the porch.

"Sloan, I'm home!" she called out, expecting him to come out of the shadows to greet her. "Sorry I'm so late, but . . ."

She looked around, knowing all the while that if he had been on the porch she couldn't have missed him, not even in the dim twilight. All she saw was the big clay pot of Swedish ivy she had put out for a little late sun before she went into town for groceries.

"Sloan?" She spoke louder now, then paused, listening for an answer. "Now, where can he have gotten to?"

She went down the steps and walked back to his car. It was a silly move to peek inside, as if he might have materialized there suddenly. If he had been in the car, even if he'd dozed off for a little nap until she got back, there was no way he could have slept through all her calling.

There was no reason to feel so panicky over not finding him where she expected. He was a grown man who was perfectly capable of taking care of himself. This was Taos—it was safe here. She squelched the faint niggle of unease that revived old fears of loss and danger.

Nothing was going to go wrong. Not again. She turned in a slow circle, looking in all directions for some sign of him. Nothing. Maybe he just went for a walk, she thought, wanting to listen to the voice of reason. It was certainly a perfect evening to wander around. The air was cool and laden with the scent of sage and pine, with the slightest hint of fall curling through the fragrant breeze.

With newfound optimism, Jesse retrieved the two bags of groceries from her car and went inside the house. If Sloan was out walking, he would probably be hungry when he got back. He was going to be surprised to find that they were going to eat here tonight, especially when he saw that she was doing all the cooking.

She hoped she wouldn't mess up the dinner. Bobbie had arranged the menu and made out the shopping list, and they had gone over how and when to do each thing at least a dozen times. With bakery-made bread sticks and pesto sauce from the deli, how hard could it be to cook the pasta and toss a salad? Bobbie had assured her that it would be almost as easy as heating up a frozen dinner, but Jesse had her doubts.

She got out the plastic bags of lettuce, peppers and cherry tomatoes and carried them to the sink. As she rinsed and cored the lettuce she glanced out the back window, noticing that the glorious pinks and reds of the sunset were fading into more muted purple and blues. Then, outlined against the pale, graying skyline, she saw the figure of a man. Sloan.

She recognized him immediately, though he was at the far reach of her vision, standing by the old Indian burial mound. Even from this distance there was no mistaking him. The width of his shoulders, the angle of his head, tilted as he watched the setting sun, the straight military line of his back—she could have picked out his silhouette from that of a thousand men of identical height and coloring. It was incredible to find he had carved such a strong image of himself in her mind in such a short time.

Jesse felt a curiously bittersweet ache. Never before had she been so completely conscious of the intimate details of a man—how he walked, how the pauses in his speech became longer any time he was nervous or worried, how he fought the urge to smile. She had never known how it felt to live for a man's smile, not even with Michael.

Jesse caught her breath, stunned at what she was admitting to herself—love. Despite all the problems it might cause and all the guilt it aroused in her, she was falling in love with J. Sloan Lassiter.

What if he didn't feel the same way? What if it was a totally one-sided passion? But she had seen the way he looked at her. This situation was far from one-sided.

There was something between them that he felt as strongly as she did. He might not love her, but he felt something for her—something strong enough to draw him here every weekend. Each time he came back, they broke through another barrier in getting to know each other.

Lately Jesse had begun to feel a little uncomfortable about discussing Michael when her dreams were filled with images of Sloan. He had never said it bothered him to think about her and Michael, but she was getting pretty good at reading the stony set of his jaw and the glacial expression in his eyes when he was ready to change the subject.

She didn't mean to keep dragging her husband's name into things, but it was such a habit of such long standing, that sometimes she did it without realizing it until it was too late. Michael had been a part of her life, not just her husband. For far longer than she had been his wife, she had been his best friend and confidante. She had very few memories that weren't linked to Michael.

She was having trouble dealing with her feelings for Sloan, here and now, without having to make unfair comparisons or judgments. In fact, although he avoided talking about it, it was evident that Sloan was having his own difficulties coping with guilt over being with her, even as a friend.

The last remnants of daylight were fading fast, and still Sloan had made no move to come back to the house. She couldn't see him anymore in the darkness, but she could almost feel his loneliness and pain across the short distance separating them.

Jesse wanted to go to him, to stand with him in the dark, to let him know that he never had to be alone again. She gave in to the impulse, putting down the vegetables and switching off the oven and the stove. Moments later, she slipped out the back door and hurried to join him.

SLOAN HEARD JESSE'S footsteps. He'd done pretty well so far at keeping things on an even keel with her, but it was getting harder all the time to remember why he was here. Damned if he was going to make a fool of himself tonight.

"Why, hello, Mr. Lassiter. Fancy running into you in a place like this." He liked hearing the teasing lilt in her voice. "It's not exactly a happening night on the town, is it?"

"I've seen bigger crowds."

"Yes, it is a little quiet tonight," she agreed, straight-faced. "If we stick around until the moon comes up, you might get to meet our most famous regular."

"Silver Wolf?"

"So you know about Silver Wolf, too," she said, shaking her head in amazement. "I'm beginning to think that Michael told you every single detail of his whole life."

"We had a long time to talk, Jess," he replied, turning to watch her make her way up the slight incline to the top of the rock-strewn mound. "He told me how digging in this old place made up his mind about what he wanted to do as a career. Every time he found a bone or picked out a piece of chipped flint, he said he could just imagine the ghost of Silver Wolf looking over his shoulder."

"That sounds like Michael." Her voice was wistful and tender. After a pause she continued, "So, tell me, have you run into any restless spirits around here?"

"I wasn't looking for spirits, restless or otherwise," he answered curtly. "I just needed to think. But this isn't the place for it. I don't have any business being here."

She had been walking closer to him, but stopped short at the hint of anger in his voice. God, he hated to be so moody. It was just hard hearing her talk about Michael. Every time she said his name her voice changed, dropped into that soft, sad tone, and he could tell she was back in time, thinking of when she had been with her husband. And every time that had happened lately, he had wanted to grab her and shake her until she came back to him, until that look was gone from her eyes—until she stopped thinking about a dead man.

He couldn't see her eyes in the darkness, but he could tell she was unhappy. The silence grew into a deafening roar. Sloan cursed under his breath, damning his stubborn attitude to hell and back. There was no reason for Jesse to have to be uncomfortable because of his jealousy of a ghost. He searched for words, deciding it was up to him to get the conversation back on a polite level.

"Of course, from all I hear, spirits are pretty choosy about the company they hang out with. It could be that they don't take kindly to strangers disturbing their home. Maybe I've frightened them away."

"Maybe you have. Lord knows, you're good at keeping people at arm's length. It probably works on ghosts, too."

"What is that supposed to mean?"

"Oh, I don't know," she said. "Don't pay any attention to me, right now. There's just something about being out here that's making me a little jittery."

"Yeah. Michael laughed about scaring you with his stories. He said you were an easy audience. Tell me, are you really afraid of this place?"

"Not really. Michael loved the legend about the ghosts of dead warriors guarding the sacred burial grounds, but I never saw anything scarier than a lizard out there."

"But you *are* frightened. I can feel it." He reached out, tentatively, brushing her shoulder with his fingertips. Even through the fabric of her shirt he could feel the faint trembling of her muscles. "You live by this place all the time. You see it every day. How can you still be so nervous?"

"Don't be ridiculous, Sloan. I'm not afraid of an old pile of rocks and bones. I'm not a child anymore."

"Then what is it, Jesse?" He was insistent. "Don't try to tell me you aren't afraid of something. You're shaking."

He put a hand on each shoulder, turning her to face him. In the light of the rising moon, her hair was a veil of pale silver. He could see her face clearly enough to catch the unease in her eyes before she ducked her chin and looked away. When she tried to shrug off his hands and move away, he tightened his fingers, keeping her gently but firmly in his grasp.

"Talk to me, Jesse. What are you so afraid of?"

"Afraid isn't exactly the word," she hedged. "Let's go in and have a nice dinner, and then maybe later we can try to talk about things."

"Maybe you could give me a clue about what 'things' you have on your mind so I can think about it for a while," he suggested. "I like the idea that you want to talk to me. It makes me think you're beginning to trust me—at least a little."

"More than a little, and you know it. I can hardly believe how much I've come to count on these weekends." Her voice was soft, showing equal parts of hope and regret. "You've been so good to look in on me."

"Yeah, it's been a real hardship, honey." His tone was light, belittling his efforts. "I hate having to spend time with a beautiful woman when I could be doing something really interesting."

"Thank you for saying that. It's very kind."

"I'm not seeing you out of kindness, Jesse. Don't make me out to be some kind of Boy Scout."

"I know you promised Michael you'd look after me, but—"

"Is that what you wanted to talk about? Michael again?" He heard the edge of disappointment sharpening his tone, but he didn't seem able to do anything to hide it. "What else can I tell you that we haven't covered a dozen times over the last few weeks?"

"Never mind, Sloan. Let's just go on back to the house."

"No, let's not. I'd just as soon get whatever is on your mind out of the way right now."

"It's...it's going to be hard for me to say very clearly." She scuffed at the ground with the toe of her shoe, sending a cascade of pebbles clattering. "It isn't... simple. In fact, I'm not sure the whole thing wouldn't be better off left alone."

"Why don't you just talk to me about whatever it is? Give me a chance to decide what I'm ready for?"

"I don't think we're ready to have this conversation, Sloan. Either of us. I really think we should go in now, and talk later."

She looked up at him, and suddenly he was as skittish as she about the wisdom of going on with their discussion. Hell, he wasn't exactly sure what it was they were on the verge of tackling, but judging from the fear in her eyes and the knot in his stomach, it was something pretty damned important.

"Waiting a couple of hours isn't going to make anything easier to handle, Jesse. Something is going on between us, something that we can't keep avoiding—not if we're going to be comfortable around each other."

"Do I make you uncomfortable, Sloan? I'd hate if it you didn't feel at home when you're here. Michael would have wanted—"

"Oh, for Christ's sake!" he swore. "Do you think we could get through just ten minutes without bringing Michael into the conversation?"

"Not if we really are going to talk about what we need to," she said, reaching out to lay her hand on his arm. "We've got to talk about our feelings for Michael ... and about how he's affecting our feelings for each other."

"I don't think I want to get into this right now. We're getting along fine the way things are without—"

"Without what, Sloan?" Jesse pressed him for an answer. "Without admitting that what we're feeling is more than friendship? Or am I alone in the things I'm wanting from you?"

"Don't push me, Jess. I can't let myself want you."

"Because of Michael."

Sloan's blood froze at her words. He had always heard the expression, but until now it had always seemed to be just another exaggeration. Now, though, he felt dread numbing his heart. All it took was hearing Michael's name from her lips. *She belonged to Michael.*

"You were Michael's wife. That's part of it."

"No, Sloan. That's *all* of it," she said earnestly. "If we didn't have Michael between us, what would you want? Would you be standing politely beside me in the moonlight, avoiding my slightest touch?" She flexed her fingers into the warmth of his forearm, digging in her fingernails with just enough force for emphasis. "Or would you take me in your arms and hold me?"

"Ah, Jesse," he breathed through gritted teeth. "Don't do this to me. Neither of us is ready for the kind of trouble you're stirring up."

"I don't want trouble. I only want to hold you. I want to know what it would be like to kiss you."

"For God's sake, Jesse," he groaned. "You don't know what you're doing to me."

"I know what you do to me."

Jesse stepped closer to him, so close that they were standing eye to eye. For a moment she just stood there, watching him without trying to hide the desire in her eyes. It was all he could do to keep from pulling her into his arms and covering her soft, full mouth with his own.

Sloan ached with the need to touch her, yet he willed himself to stay still. If he made a move in her direction, it would be both their undoing.

"Please, talk to me," she whispered. "Let me know if I'm making a complete fool of myself. Have I misunderstood what's happening between us? Don't you want me, after all?"

"This isn't a question of wanting, honey. If that's all it was, we would have been all over each other the first time I had you in my arms."

"What is it, then? I don't have a lot of experience at this sort of thing, you know." She lowered her lids in embarrassment. "Actually, you're the first man I've even wanted to be with, since . . . ."

She didn't finish the thought. She didn't have to. They both filled in Michael's name. Sloan was beginning to wish he had never heard that name. If only he could look at her without the old memories of Michael's smile when he spoke her name. If . . .

"There's too much in the way, Jesse. We'd tear each other up trying not to say his name."

"I'm not used to begging, Sloan."

He could hear the hurt, but, God help him, anything he did right now was only going to make things harder later. He couldn't find the words to turn her away. No matter how smart it would be, he couldn't say he didn't want her.

Just when he thought he couldn't hold on for another second, she broke the stalemate. She shook back her hair and took two steps backward, severing the bond of sexual tension that had held them captive. She straightened her spine and lifted her chin with defiant grace.

"All right, Sloan. If that's how you want it."

"That's how it has to be."

"Fine." She was calm and reasonable. Her deadly calm was overlaid with a polite veneer that would have been appropriate with a total stranger.

"I'm going inside and finish making dinner. It should be ready in a few minutes."

"Would you rather I go now?"

"Of course not." She told the lie without hesitation, but he knew it had cost her. "There's no reason we can't be civilized about this, is there? There's no sense in wasting a perfectly good meal."

"Come on, honey. You don't have to pretend with me. I'll understand if you tell me to hit the road."

"Don't be ridiculous," she said without inflection. "After all, I'm not the first woman on earth to be turned down in a situation like this."

She spun on her heel and walked away without another glance, leaving him staring after her in silent frustration. He hated hearing that cold, jaded tone, but he admired her guts. It grated against his nerves to see her try to be something she wasn't, and she was the furthest thing on earth from the haughty ice queen who had suddenly taken over.

He wanted to go after her, or at least to shout at her to drop the deep-freeze treatment. Instead, he balled his hands into fists and watched her without saying a word until she entered the house and shut the door behind her.

"Let her go, Lassiter. Let her go, and pray to God she can hold a grudge."

He followed the path back to the house. If he had an ounce of sense, he would drive out of here without getting within a hundred feet of the woman.

"Hell, man, if you had a single brain cell working, you wouldn't even think about staying around here." He reached the door and stood there for a minute, good judgment warring with the need to see her again, to spend one last night with her before he left. One last night.

"Yeah, and who are you trying to kid, Lassiter? Your brain hasn't been working since the day you first saw her picture."

He took one last breath of the cool night air and stepped inside.

10

THE MEAL WAS A DISMAL failure.

Jesse nibbled at a breadstick and pushed her salad around her plate. For the life of her, she had no real idea how the food turned out. Even if she'd been blessed with a gourmet's palate instead of her own plebeian taste buds, she was too conscious of the man sitting across the table from her to pay much attention to what she was eating.

Either her cooking was worse than she thought, or Sloan's appetite was as much affected by their spat as hers. He'd made a respectable dent in his serving of pasta, but she could tell from the mechanical way he ate that he wasn't really enjoying it. The level of conversation was somewhere between stilted and nonexistent. Finally, Jesse gave up trying to maintain the facade that they were being civilized.

"I'm sorry, but I can't do this anymore." She stood and picked up her plate. "If you want to sit there and pretend you can eat, go right ahead. This is a bunch of garbage."

"Hey, it's not that bad. I take back all the cracks about your cooking."

Jesse glared at him. If he thought she was going to be diverted from the problem between them with his half-baked attempts at humor, he was not only a coward, he was a fool.

"Sloan, tell me something."

"Sure."

"No, this is serious. It may not be easy for either of us to talk about, but can we please try to forget about being polite and cautious and have a few minutes when we try talking to each other honestly?"

"I'll try. Let me tell you right up front, though—I'm not a real open kind of guy. It may be trendy right now to sort of let it all hang out and talk about every feeling you have, but I'm not exactly comfortable with making my relationships into a topic for Oprah or Donahue."

"Is that what we have here—a relationship?"

"Call it whatever you want, Jesse. It's sure as hell something."

"I'm not any more certain how to handle this than you are, to tell the truth. In my whole life, the only other man that I ever went out with was Michael. He was everything to me."

"I thought we weren't going to talk about him again. I thought this discussion was about you and me."

"Do you think there is any way to talk about us without bringing up his name from time to time? If we don't accept what we feel about Michael, I don't think there can ever be any peace between us."

"Peace? Is that what you want from me? How about comfort, Jess? Brotherly love? Is that next on your list? If you're looking for a safe, platonic friendship where we sit around and talk about what a great guy your late husband is and go out to dinner occasionally, I think you're dealing with the wrong man."

"That's not what I mean at all. What's going on between us is not at all safe and platonic, but before we can explore what we feel for each other, we have to get past this morbid guilt trip of yours."

"My guilt trip? Is that what you think this is about?"

"Absolutely. You came here to pay your noble duty visit to the grieving widow, and then, when you felt the slightest bit of attraction to me, it threw you into a total tailspin, didn't it?"

"You don't know a damned thing about what I came here for or what I expected to find."

"Oh, no? You expected to find a sweet, innocent young thing, languishing in her bereavement. Michael always thought I was much more delicate than I really am. Is that your problem, too? Were you disappointed that I had managed to start a new life on my own?"

"No, I was real impressed by how well you were doing. If learning how to drink and party is part of this new life that you're so proud of establishing, you sure got off to a great start."

"I can't believe you're still throwing that in my face. After meeting Bobbie and Hank and listening to the whole story, how can you even mention it?"

"I know I shouldn't dwell on it," he admitted, "but it didn't get us off to a great start. You have to understand that finding you half-naked and drunk threw me for a loop. It was a very different picture from what I'd heard about from . . . from Michael." The name didn't come easily, but he managed to get it out. "I guess he did lay it on a bit thick about your being the daughter of a minister and all that stuff."

"So you came out here, expecting Rebecca of Sunnybrook Farm, and it destroyed all the pretty little images of me that you had built up in your mind. I'm a real, live woman. With real strengths, real weaknesses. Don't try and make me whoever you and Michael wanted me to be."

"You have it all worked out, don't you? Well, lady, if I told you the things I thought about you, the way I imagined you would be, you'd never be able to handle it. You'd be shocked out of your little Puritan skull."

"Give me a chance to make that choice. All I need is another man to protect me and save me from having to make up my own mind. I was getting tired of that with Michael, and I won't start the same old song and dance with you."

"Michael worshiped you. All he wanted was to take care of you. That's why he asked me to check on you . . . see if you needed any help."

"And that's what all this attention is about? I don't want you to pick up where Michael left off." Jesse was emphatic. "I don't need to be rescued, and I sure don't need to be babied anymore."

"There's a difference between protecting and babying, Jesse. I only want to see that you are taken care of. I want to look after you."

"You don't have the guts to admit that's only a part of what you want from me, do you, Sloan? Michael was overprotective, but at least he knew what he wanted from me. Michael and I had our problems, but—"

"We may need to talk about him, but I don't want to hear about your problems with him."

"And why shouldn't you hear my version of it? It seems to me that my husband went into great detail about our marriage. Surely there can't be much Michael didn't tell you about me."

"That's different. You don't understand how things were—how important it was to him to keep his memories alive."

"Make me understand, Sloan. Tell me how it was."

"It was death by inches. Losing a little part of your life every day, knowing it could never be recaptured. Wondering if anyone still remembered your name or your face. Wondering how much they had changed. Michael was afraid that if he didn't keep your memory alive, he wouldn't be alive himself."

"So he talked about me to you?"

"Yeah." Sloan looked down at his hands. "He talked about you most of all. He talked and I listened. I met you in that cell. I watched you grow during those months, brought to life by Michael's memories. I learned to live in his family."

"And what about your family, Sloan? Did you share all of your memories with Michael?"

"My family is all dead."

"Oh, Sloan. I'm sorry. I didn't mean to—"

"No problem. It was just my father and me, and we were never really close enough to quite make it as a family anyhow. I didn't grow up in a perfect family like you guys."

"Your fantasies are showing again. Don't you know that there's no such thing as a perfect family, Sloan? Certainly not ours."

"That's not how Michael remembered it. I'm surprised they didn't put you all on television." He held up a hand to stop her attempt to argue the point. "Okay, it might not have been 'Father Knows Best,' but it sounded like what I'd longed for all my life."

"I'd like to hear about your family. Where did you grow up?"

"Everywhere. Typical service brat. If I'd had anything worth talking about, I wouldn't have needed Michael's stories so much. You see, at first I thought it was a harmless fantasy. He would talk and I would close my eyes and listen, trying to imagine what it was like to be a part of it."

"I still don't see why it bothers you so much. It was harmless—"

"Harmless? Sweet Jesus, what a joke! I began to live in those stories. I lived to hear them, over and over again. After a while it was like his memories were my own, his family, my own." He looked at her then, and the blue flame of his eyes burned into her soul. "His wife . . ."

Suddenly she understood.

"You pretended that I was . . . that we were . . ."

"I did more than pretend, Jesse. I lusted after you. I *coveted* you. Every time he said your name, I blanked him out of the picture so I could have you to myself."

"You were under a lot of pressure, Sloan. Michael was coping the only way he could—by talking about us. Don't blame yourself for finding a way to get through it, too. You had a right to—"

"I had no right, Jess. That's a bunch of bull. Michael was my friend, my only real friend. Don't tell me I had a right to fantasize about his wife."

"It was only a fantasy. Do you think I spent the last three years without thinking a single thought about having someone to hold me?"

"I don't believe you spent your nights dreaming about another woman's husband. You must have dreamed of Michael."

"Mostly. I still do sometimes, but—"

"That's just great. We can compare notes sometime." He was suddenly angry with her. "I don't think this is a good idea. All this honesty and sharing of our erotic fantasies is a little more than I bargained for."

"We have to talk about it, Sloan. I want—"

"You want?" He looked at her with an intensity that was frightening. "You want? Hell, lady, I don't think you have any idea what it is to want."

"Don't I?" She backed up against the counter and braced her hands behind her, needing the support to keep her shaking knees from giving way under the wave of longing that washed over her. "I don't think I've ever wanted anything as much as I want you right now."

In an instant he crossed the few steps separating them, knocking over his chair, sending it crashing to the floor. She knew the very second he touched her that he was burning out of control. When he grasped her upper arms and pulled her against him, she didn't make any effort to resist.

He brought his mouth to within an inch of hers and then stopped short of making contact, holding her so tightly she didn't know where he stopped and she started. Her heart pounded with excitement heightened by fear—fear that he would regain his senses before he kissed her. She felt the heat of his breath and her own breathing quickened to match his passion-ragged gasps, but still he held on to his control with an iron will. She whimpered in frustration.

"Don't think, Sloan. Feel."

"This is wrong, Jess." He shook with the strain of keeping them apart, struggling against the inevitable tide. "We shouldn't—"

"Please, Sloan," she begged. "Forget about what was and what should be. Let it happen. Let *us* happen."

His answer was a low growl deep in his throat. Then, before she could lose her nerve, she closed her eyes and leaned toward him, and they embraced.

The first kiss was surprisingly gentle. After the weeks of longing and denial, it was devastating in its sweetness. His mouth settled over hers without demanding her response, instead tasting and inviting her to open to him. She responded without hesitation, parting her lips and melting into his arms.

He outlined her upper lip with the tip of his tongue, delicately, like an artist making the first tentative strokes on a pristine canvas.

Jesse quivered, feeling each stroke, each nibble with exquisite awareness. Her skin was supremely sensitized to his touch, to the warmth of his breath as it feathered across her cheeks and into her hair.

She felt strangely pliant, malleable under his hands as he touched her. His beautiful hands encircled her waist and slid a leisurely path up to her neck, leaving an awakening hunger in every muscle on the way. One hand stopped behind her neck, tangling in the weight of her hair.

With his other hand he made love to her face, tracing the curve of her ear and setting off a shimmer of heat as he drew impossibly tiny circles on the soft, hidden skin just behind it. He made a leisurely trail down her neck until his fingers reached the collar of her shirt. Jesse held her breath, paralyzed with anticipation of the moment when they would slip inside her blouse. But then he returned his hand to her chin and tipped her head back a bit, opening his fingers over her skin.

It was shattering to be held so literally in the cradle of his hands. His thumb gently rubbed the underside of her chin, while his fingers caressed the hollow of her cheek. Jesse had never thought of her face as an erogenous zone, but she found herself pressing her cheek upward against his gentle stroking, lifting her chin to prolong each butterfly-soft touch. Just when she thought nothing could be more sensual, more exciting, he proved her wrong.

It was a simple action, nothing outrageous or kinky, but it was shocking in its impact on her body. He touched their joined lips with the tip of his forefinger and began to lightly stroke the corner of her mouth. Then, without breaking the kiss, he slid his finger just inside her lower lip, into the slick wetness there. Her heart quickened as he lightly tested the sharp edge of her teeth before withdrawing.

"Sloan," she whispered against his lips, unable to suppress the need to say his name aloud. "Oh, Sloan. What are you doing to me?"

"I think I'm going to make love to you, despite all my efforts to the contrary." He sounded ardent, yet still none too pleased with the situation. "Unless you've changed your mind..." He nipped her lip with his teeth with just enough force to turn her insides to jelly. "Would you like me to stop now?"

"I don't think I ever want you to stop." Jesse turned her head to the side to place a slow, openmouthed kiss on the hand that still cradled her face. "You have the most incredible hands. I noticed that the first time I met you. Sometimes..." She swallowed, hating the unsteady note in her voice, then tried again. "Sometimes I would wonder... I'd want..." She felt the flush in her cheeks and closed her eyes to hide her sudden embarrassment. "Never mind. Just kiss me again."

"In a minute. After you tell me." He stood without moving, not attempting to rush her, until she found the courage to look at him once more. "I need for you to tell me what you feel, what you want. Trust me enough to tell me what you want."

"I don't know if I can." She was embarrassed at her own fear. "I'm not used to talking about what I need—"

"And I'm not used to caring enough to ask." Sloan looked a little unsettled himself, but he pushed her to continue. "But, for once in my life, I do care—enough to want to make it everything you want. Can you tell me? What do you want?"

It took all the strength she had to look him in the eye and answer. Her voice was low and tremulous.

"I want to feel your hands on me."

"Thank God for small favors, sweetness. If that's what you need, then neither of us has a thing to worry about."

11

VERY SLOWLY, VERY deliberately, Sloan took one step back from her, but without breaking the connection between them. Beginning at the top of her head, he caressed her, reading her with his hands.

"I've waited forever to do this," he said gravely. "If you knew how hard I've tried to keep my hands out of your hair...how hard I've tried to keep myself from touching you—"

"Stop trying to talk yourself out of things, Sloan." Jesse reveled in the luxury of his gentle touch, but she was aching for more. "Don't just keep on dreaming of what you want. Reach out and take it."

His fingers clenched in her hair, not hurting, but with an intensity that betrayed his need. Knotting his fingers in the silky strands, he pulled her head back to expose the vulnerable line of her throat.

Jesse closed her eyes and waited for the touch of his lips on her skin, anticipating the moment of contact. Yet, no amount of anticipation could have prepared her for the way her heart seemed to stop at the first brush of his open mouth on her neck. The thrilling scratchiness of his faint beard stubble reminded her of how a man's touch could set up a slow-burning heat low in her body.

He trailed his mouth down her neck, burrowing his way into the open neckline of her shirt until he found her breasts. She shuddered as the heat of his caresses branded her even through the lacy fabric of her bra. She lifted her arms to embrace him. Her fingers encircled his head, threading through the dark tangle of his hair, stroking the corded muscles at the back of his neck, unashamedly pressing his face more intimately against her.

"More," she urged. "I want more.... I want you to make love to me."

"That's all I needed to hear," he said in a voice that shook with emotion. He pulled her fully into his arms, fitting her body from hip to chest against his own. "My God, Jesse. It seems like I've been waiting forever to hear you say those words. And now..."

There was no more need for words. Jesse read all he had to say in the blue-hot flame of his eyes. Then he closed his eyes and lowered his head to slant his lips over hers, sealing them together in a kiss.

From that moment, things would never be the same. They both knew and accepted and gave themselves up to the power of mutual, sensual insanity. As they remained locked within the magic circle of their joining, lips and tongues mated, questing for a satiation of hunger. There was no thought or reason, only the need to taste and learn all the hidden, secret places. The sensation became the moment as everything—every breath, every nuance—pulled them deeper into the whirlpool of desire.

They gave to each other all the pent-up longing they had tried to suppress, holding back nothing as they strained to get closer. Sloan gathered her into his arms, holding her so tightly there were no secrets between them despite the barriers of their clothing. He was fully erect. He insinuated his hips into the cradle of her thighs, and she welcomed the unrestrained, aggressive rocking motion.

Even in the middle of the maelstrom, there was no doubt that he was giving her a choice—one last chance to call it off. Jesse knew she could stop him even now, but instead, she arched her hips to fit even more closely together and moaned her need into the wet cavern of his mouth. He growled low in his throat and matched the rhythm of his hips to the give and take of their kiss.

Yet it wasn't enough. Each kiss demanded another, more intimate one. Each brush of a hand against heated flesh stoked the flame higher. Each instance of feeding fed the hunger, setting up an ever-greater demand for completion.

With a desperation so intense it wiped out patience and any thought of finesse, Sloan began to remove her clothes, cursing as his fingers shook and fumbled with the buttons on her shirt. Her hands were no less steady as she matched his actions, caught up in the frenzy of the moment. Her hands finally created an opening large enough to slip inside his shirt, and she shivered at the thrill of trailing her fingers through the dark tangle of hair that covered his chest. She pushed the open shirt back to expose a greater expanse of his chest and the hard-muscled fullness of his broad shoulders.

He helped her, shrugging the shirt off with an impatience born of desperation. It fell to the floor at the same time as her blouse, as if the two movements were synchronized by long practice. In a matter of seconds they were both bare to the waist.

Jesse opened her arms and reached out for him, eagerly. Her mind reeled at the very thought of what it would be like to press her naked breasts into his wiry chest hair.

At the first brush of skin on bare skin, she felt the imprint of each dark curl, branding her with hot sweet fire. The burst of wanting was so intense that she caught her breath and whimpered softly, barely containing her need to cry out his name. Then he pulled her even closer, pressing them so tightly together that she knew the full strength and power of his need. He buried his face in the crook of her neck and spoke to her, punctuating his words with soft, biting kisses on the delicate skin.

"I want you, Jess.... The rest doesn't matter anymore—not any of it...." He licked his way down the curve of her throat to her breasts. "Nothing matters except you ... except being with you ... inside you."

Jesse thought she would die from the pleasure. His hands stroked at her clothes as he whispered his need, making it seem the most natural thing in the world to be lifted onto a kitchen countertop and undressed in a few deft moves.

"You have the most incredible legs," he said as he removed her lace panties, sliding the scrap of fabric down their length. "Long and smooth and tanned. I've dreamed of the time when I could feel them wrapped around me...."

"Ah, God, yes," he moaned as she locked her legs around his waist. "That's it, exactly, honey. Let me feel you against my skin. Move with me."

The fever-hot flesh of his body seared the insides of her thighs and arms as she clung to him. All she could think of was the delicious waves of pleasure that shimmered through her body.

The rough denim of his jeans waistband was less pleasant than his skin, but even it was exciting as she settled herself more fully against him. Even through the cloth, she felt the ridged hardness of his body. She rubbed herself against his erection.

"Don't do that too much, sweetness," he growled, the immediate upward thrust of his hips belying his order. "Not unless you're ready for it to all be over before I get undressed."

"Then you'd better get undressed in a hurry, Sloan. Just touching you like this, feeling you between my legs, is driving me crazy." She flushed as he looked into her face, knowing he had to see how close she was to the edge already. "I'm sorry to be so . . ."

"So what, Jess?" He flexed himself against her, still watching her closely. "So hot? So ready?"

He slipped one hand between them and cupped her mound, finding the slick, hidden wetness with skilled fingers. Jesse stiffened as he found the tiny nub of flesh and stroked it with a loving tenderness. She leaned forward to sink her teeth gently into his shoulder.

She concentrated on the salty flavor of his skin and the clean, woodsy tang of his cologne, not wanting to give in to her approaching climax. She tried to hold back the rising tide of her passion, to allow herself a few more moments of the bittersweet yearning his touch invoked.

"Wait, Sloan."

"Wait for what, Jess?" The urgent movement of his hand slowed and lightened the pressure until it was only a nerve-shattering vibration. "I'm a little short on control right now, so talk quick."

"I don't want to talk. I want to make love."

"We *are* making love, honey."

"More." She let her head fall backward and separated their upper bodies enough to give him access to her breasts. "I want to feel everything," she said.

"Is this what you want?" He kissed her, tracing the dark pink areola before flicking the erect nipple with the tip of his tongue. "Or this?" He drew her into the warmth of his mouth, tugging and suckling at her breast until she was an inch away from delicious insanity. "Tell me what I can do to make it good for you."

"It *is* good. So good," she encouraged, guiding him to her other breast. "I don't want you to stop, but if I don't feel you inside me soon, I think I'll scream."

"I think I'll get to hear you scream either way, love."

His laugh was one of joy, low and sexy, rumbling up from deep within his chest. He nuzzled the valley between her breasts, giving her a kiss there before setting her on the edge of the countertop between his open legs. As she watched, he unsnapped his jeans and hooked his fingers inside both jeans and underwear, removing them together in a single, efficient movement. He stood before her without embarrassment, letting her look at him with the longing he had shown her moments earlier.

"You are so beautiful."

"I think that's supposed to be my line," he said gruffly.

"But you are beautiful, Sloan." Jesse reached out to touch him, lightly trailing her fingertips through the black thicket of pubic hair before closing her hand around the fullness of his penis. "Does it bother you that I like to look at you?"

She moved her hand carefully upward, then back down all the way to his body, encouraged by the quick inhalation of air between his clenched teeth.

"Do you want me to pretend that it doesn't excite me as much to touch you as to be touched by you?"

"Hell, no," he whispered. "I want you to do whatever you feel like doing. I don't want you to pretend anything with me, ever." He reached down and covered her hand with his own, then continued raggedly. "But, in spite of that, I wish you'd stop this for now."

"It doesn't feel like you want me to stop." She stroked him again, and again, watching his muscles tense and flex with each repetition. "And I like being able to make you feel this way."

"Don't push it, baby," he warned. "If you want me to be able to make love to you, I'd suggest you at least slow down. Give me a minute to—"

"I understand, Sloan," she said, flushing that he had to be the one to be responsible.

Thank goodness he was able to think clearly when she hadn't even given a thought to protection. It had been a long time since she had been in a situation where she had to deal with this problem. Things had gone too far to be shy about practicalities.

"Can you reach your wallet?"

"Now, why the hell would I want my wallet at a time like this?"

"Isn't that where guys keep them?"

"Keep what?"

"You know, Sloan. Protection."

"Pro—" He stopped suddenly, staring at her in horror. "You're talking about contraceptives. You think I'm carrying a condom in there?"

She nodded.

He cursed.

"Damn it. I never thought of that at all." Sloan reached out and touched her cheek. "You aren't on the Pill or anything?"

"I haven't had any reason to be."

"But it's been years. Surely you—"

"I didn't. Not ever." It seemed important to make things clear to him, so she repeated herself. "Not ever. I never met anyone I wanted to be with. Until now."

"Damn it to hell and back."

"I'm sorry, Sloan." Jesse recoiled from the anger in his voice. "I know you must be frustrated, but please don't be mad at me. I'm so sorry."

"You're sorry?" Sloan studied her face and the anger drained out of him as she watched and was replaced by a fierce tenderness. He lifted her off the counter and took her into his arms, holding on to her as if she were his lifeline. "You don't have a blasted thing to be sorry for, angel. I'm not mad at you. Just disappointed for a minute."

"I didn't want to disappoint you—"

"That's the last thing I'd say you did. It's not your fault, Jess." He straightened her hair with his hands, and touched a wild curl behind her ear. "Now that I know the problem, everything will work out okay."

"Are you sure?"

"Absolutely. Trust me on this one."

He kissed her on the forehead, then covered her mouth with his own, tenderly at first, but with a growing passion that left no doubt of his desire. His tongue searched out her own and as they touched, the embers of wanting burst back into flame. They stroked each other as they kissed.

Jesse held on tightly to Sloan, reeling under the ravenous onslaught of his mouth, literally clinging to him to keep from sliding to the floor and pulling him down with her. Yet, despite the boneless weakness in her legs, she returned his kisses with eagerness, drawing his tongue deeper and swirling her own around it, urging him to establish a deep, stroking rhythm in her mouth.

Her body screamed for release as the kissing and petting became a torment of denial. She struggled up from the smoky, erotic spell he was weaving about her, seeking an escape from the pleasure that was becoming an exquisite and beautiful pain.

"Please, Sloan. Stop now. Now, while I have the strength to end it. If we don't stop now, I'll end up begging you to do something we both could regret later."

"Shh, sweetness," he soothed, even as his hands glided over her full breasts and traced the sharp curve of her waistline as if molding her out of living clay. "Let me take care of you. I promise you aren't in any danger from me. Not any kind of danger, at all."

"But we can't do this. It's not as if we are a couple of kids who don't know any better. It's too big a risk for—"

"You're right about one thing, Jess." He stopped her argument by touching her lips with his forefinger, sliding his finger back and forth to capture the sheen of moisture left there from his kisses. "We aren't kids. There are options in lovemaking that kids might not think of at this point. I don't have to be inside you to make love to you. This isn't just about screwing, baby. This is about sharing."

"I want to share myself with you, Sloan. I want to give you what you need, but I don't know if I can do this."

"Do what?"

"Do . . . Do whatever you want to do instead of . . ."

"Hmm, that sounds interesting." He smiled and cupped his hand over her pubic bone, setting off an alarming chain of shivers deep inside her. "Exactly what do you think I have in mind?"

Jesse swallowed hard, seeing the light of need and willingness in his eyes. It was frightening how much she wanted him. It was also frightening to know that her sexual experience, besides being very limited, was also boringly conventional.

"I'm not sure, but I think you should know, I'm probably not... That is, I don't really know how to..." Jesse gave up trying to make excuses, but she did want him to know she was only lacking in experience, not in nerve. "What do you want me to do?"

"Did you ever hear the old phrase, 'Just lean back and enjoy it'?"

"I never thought of it in terms of the kitchen," she replied, looking around them doubtfully. "Should we go upstairs?"

"Maybe later. Right now, I'm not in the mood to wait any longer." He reached behind her and opened a cabinet door briefly, making a sound of satisfaction as he found what he was searching for. "I knew I saw this here the other day. Now, just let me get it open."

"Vegetable oil? What are you going to do with that?"

Jesse didn't have long to wait for an answer. Before she even thought of stopping him, Sloan had unscrewed the lid and tipped the bottle to one side, pouring a thin drizzle of the light, golden oil on her breasts. He watched them as the oil slick spread, becoming even more liquid as it achieved body heat, and dripped from her nipples to fall in slow motion onto the flat plane of her belly.

She closed her eyes and concentrated on tracing the path of the river of oil as it spread, admitting to herself that it felt wonderfully decadent. Although it lacked the delicate perfume of her favorite bath soap, the odor was surprisingly faint and inoffensive.

"Now, relax, and let me take care of you."

Jesse opened her eyes to find Sloan had put down the bottle and was watching her intently, his darkly handsome face set in an expression she could only describe as intently erotic. He certainly didn't look as playful as she would have expected from a naked man armed with a bottle of cooking oil. In fact, he was deadly serious.

"What about you?" she asked uncertainly. "Shouldn't I rub some of that stuff on you, too?"

"I fully expect I'll have some on me before we're through, but for now—" he rubbed one finger over her lips, leaving them shining "—I just want to take pleasure in giving you pleasure."

"I'm not sure exactly what you want me to do," she said, gasping slightly as his hands began to work the slippery surface of her skin. "Are we supposed to be giving each other a massage or—"

"We are supposed to make each other feel wonderful, sweet Jesse. That's the only rule here, except ensuring your protection. Anything we feel like doing is part of making love to each other. Anything you want . . ."

His voice was as smooth and light as the oil, as seductive as the tantalizing glide of his beautiful hands as he outlined each of her hipbones. Jesse watched him through half-open eyes, falling so deeply under the spell of his ministrations that she could feel each nerve, each pore of her skin as it came to life beneath his touch. For the moment, that was all her world—watching his hands on her body. They were browner than her skin and the contrast was as beautiful to see as it was to feel. Almost.

Then his hands began to knead the insides of her legs in tiny, concentric circles, beginning with the softness behind her knees. Jesse couldn't stop herself from tensing as he moved slowly upward, inch by fraction of an inch, moving ever closer to the sweet ache between her thighs. She found herself lifting her hips in a rhythmic pattern, enjoying the growing tension, and each motion brought her nearer to the reward of his loving hands.

The waiting was both infuriating and tantalizing. Without any sense of shyness or shame, she opened herself to him, inviting the deeper touch, willing the sensual invasion. When he slid into the liquid warmth, she capitulated with a sigh of abandon.

It was all sensation, then—no thought, no real sense of reciprocation. His mouth opened over the mound of her breast and the hot, wet suckling of his lips and tongue matched the deft magic of his fingers. One hand slipped beneath her bottom, lifting her and skillfully massaging her straining muscles so that it seemed her whole body pulsated at the same rapidly accelerating pace.

She meant to enjoy his attentions for just a few short minutes until she touched him in return, but every time she tried to focus her senses to include any coherent thought, he swept her back into chaos with a deeper touch or a soul-drugging kiss.

It might have been for ten minutes or ten hours that he paid homage to her body. She glistened now with a fine sheen of perspiration, as well as the oil.

For a terrifying split second he was gone, and her eyes flew open, trying to find what had happened to break the rhythmic stroking. Before her brain could do more than register the fact that he had dropped to his knees on the floor in front of her, she felt the heat of his breath on her inner thighs. His intention was made fact before she could protest. He draped her legs over his shoulders and fitted her closely against his mouth, kissing her deeply and intimately and groaning his encouragement.

When he reached up to gently squeeze her aching breasts, Jesse lost all touch with reality. She cried his name and spun out of control into a kaleidoscope of sensual release. Her only connection with the earth was Sloan, and she clutched at him, holding on to his shoulders for dear life, burying her fingers in his hair.

When her body had passed through the gateway of ecstasy into total relaxation, he caught her and shifted her to lie in the strong haven of his arms. As she shuddered with the aftershocks of her climax, he lifted her and carried her out of the brightly lit kitchen into the quiet darkness of the hallway. They were halfway up the stairs before she recovered enough to speak.

"You don't have to carry me. I can walk."

"I wouldn't bet on it," he said in a low, indulgent growl. "Your legs are still quivering. But even if you can, that would mean I'd have to let you out of my arms, and I'm not ready to do that just yet."

"I'm not trying to escape, Sloan." Jesse tugged at the hair at the back of his neck, excited by the heated dampness there. "But I'm not exactly a featherweight for you to lug up a flight of stairs when I can walk up beside you."

"Okay. If that's what you want, I'll put you down."

Sloan shifted her in his arms until they were face-to-face, and only then did he begin to lower her to the floor. Jesse watched his eyes gleam and darken with newly intensified desire as her slippery body slid slowly and seductively down the length of his.

Without the layers of clothing between them, there was nothing to concentrate on except the delirious texture of skin against skin. Smooth feminine skin, gleaming from the coating of oil he had so lavishly applied. Hard and hair-roughened male flesh, glistening with the honest sweat of barely leashed passion. Yin and yang.

"Wait." Jesse clung to him for a moment, dizzy with the heat and scent of him, maddened by her need to be possessed totally by him and to have all of him she dared to take. "No, let's not wait." She tore herself from his arms and tugged impatiently on his hand until they reached the top of the stairs. "Come on. My bedroom is right here."

She turned and pushed open the door with one hand, still keeping the fingers of their other hands laced together. He hesitated for a moment at the threshold, then allowed himself to be drawn inside the darkened room, but the shift in his mood was obvious. It wasn't so much a cooling of physical desire as a subtle withdrawal of emotional closeness.

Jesse felt his resistance and fought to recapture the mind-boggling intimacy they had shared only moments before. She lifted his hand and brought it to her mouth, gently pressing her lips to his fingers.

"Come here," she murmured, moving closer to the bed and drawing him with her. "Let me make love to you now."

Sloan didn't move toward her as she sank down onto the softness of the bed. Instead, he tensed even more, standing beside her as if frozen in place, so still it was frightening. Jesse looked up at him in the faint light, hoping to see some trace in his eyes of love and passion, but his eyes weren't focused on her anymore. He was looking down at the picture on her bedside table—staring down into Michael's smiling blue eyes.

12

SLOAN BRACED HIMSELF against the lancing pain that cut through his chest and threatened to stop his breathing. He locked his knees and forced himself to look down at the photograph, memorizing forever the heavy silver frame gleaming dully in the dim light. It struck him as odd that even in the near darkness the picture stood out as if bathed in some unseen spotlight. The unexpected sight of Michael had hit him hard, nearly knocked him off his feet, but suddenly, as quickly as it had come, all the pain stopped.

The numbness was a blessed relief after the burst of agony. It was a survival mechanism, he thought with cool detachment; a sort of psychic shock reaction to protect him from a deep emotional wound.

"Oh, God, Sloan. I'm sorry."

He heard Jesse's voice coming through from somewhere outside, noting the anguish in her tone. He looked down at her and noticed that his fingers were still holding hers, gripping them with enough force that it had to be hurting. He knew he should let go, but somehow he lacked the power to make the thought become an action.

"I really am sorry." Jesse broke the contact for him, jerking her hand from his grasp and grabbing the picture. "This is . . . It's just . . . I didn't remember. I didn't even think about you being in here . . . seeing this."

Her arm brushed against him as she made an effort to open the bedside drawer to put the picture inside, but her hands were shaking so badly that she fumbled and dropped it. They both watched the silver frame fall— her face still twisted with guilty horror, his as white and blank as a death mask. The photograph hit the carpeted floor with a muted thud and lay between them, face up, like a live grenade.

Neither of them moved for what felt like forever. The room was filled with an unnatural quiet broken only by their quickened breathing. Michael's face alone remained unchanged, his bright and honest smile caught eternally on the glossy paper, smiling up at them without judgment or regret. Sloan felt the edge of the knife of pain again, barely pressing into his heart, exerting just enough force to remind him that he was alive. He knew it wouldn't be long before the anesthesia of shock wore off, and he had enough sanity to want to be out of this situation—hell, out of this state—before that happened.

"I'll get it," he said, breaking the silence in a voice that betrayed nothing of his torture.

He bent and picked it up, careful to keep his fingers on the metal frame. There was something about touching the picture itself that made his stomach turn. He tried not to look at her, but Jesse laid her hand on his forearm and held on until he met her gaze.

"Look at me, Sloan," she whispered. "Don't shut me out anymore."

"Okay, I'm looking at you." He glanced briefly at her as she sat, still warm and naked from his touch, and focused his eyes just above her head. "Is that better?"

"No, not like that."

"Like what?" He briefly met her gaze, not liking the way it made him feel to see the plea for understanding in their brown depths.

"Like you can't stand the sight of me. Not after what we just shared. Not after what we were going to do."

"I like the sight of you just fine." She flinched visibly at his sarcastic reply, shrinking and crossing her free hand over her bare breasts as he raked her with narrowed gaze. "It's the other sights in this room that cooled my mood a little."

"I told you that I'm sorry about the picture, Sloan, but—"

"Don't play games with me, Jesse," he snarled, anger replacing the cold deadness that had immobilized him. "It's not just the damned picture in your little shrine here that bothers me."

"Shrine?" Jesse straightened her spine, bristling at his hostile words, but not releasing her hold on his arm. "Look, I know this has upset you. It's upset both of us, but there's really no reason for you to get so hateful."

"*So hateful?*" He parroted her words back to her, his inflection making a mockery of them. "You drive me to the edge of insanity, lead me up here shaking with wanting you, then hit me in the face with this...this..."

He sputtered, searching for words, then settled for a vicious glare at the photograph before continuing. "And you think I can just stand here and keep a civil conversation going? Good Lord, lady. You don't know much about men's egos, do you?"

"I wasn't trying to play to your ego, Sloan." Jesse lifted her hand from his arm and reached out to snatch the picture from his fingers. "This has nothing to do with us. The plain truth is, I didn't think about Michael at all when I was with you, much less worry about how you'd react to seeing a photograph of him in my room."

She tried again to open the drawer, managing with still-unsteady fingers to slide it out, and deliberately put the picture away before looking back into his face. There was a trace of defiance in the lift of her chin, and the darkness of her eyes reflected a heat that was more anger than desire.

"I don't think I should have to keep apologizing for keeping a tiny part of Michael in my life."

"Oh, hell's bells, Jess. 'A little part of him.' Don't make me laugh." He grabbed her left hand and shook it in front of her face, only inches from her nose. "You still wear his ring on your finger, woman. You kiss me and beg me to make love to you and all the while you still wear his ring. How am I supposed to feel, when you touch me with his brand still on you, then bring me to your bed with him looking on, and still think I can make love to you?"

"My wedding ring?" She looked down at the gold band on her finger as if seeing it for the first time. "I've worn it so long—I never thought about it."

"That's what I'm telling you," he said in a low growl. "You haven't put any of him away. You're still married, right down to your fingertips."

"I'll take it off." She twisted at the ring, getting it halfway up her finger before he stopped her with a curse.

"Leave it alone." She stopped pulling on the wide metal band, frozen by the fury in his voice. "Don't do it for me. It isn't going to change my mind now."

He couldn't help the anger and bitterness in his tone. She was asking for too much. What the hell did she think he was made of? After all the passion and promise of their heated lovemaking, she brought him into her bedroom—not that he hadn't come all too willingly—into the bedroom that still featured a picture of her husband. How did she expect him to react?

Sloan spun on his heel and strode to the open door of the bathroom where he grabbed a bath towel and wrapped it around his hips. He yanked a second towel off the rack and walked back to the edge of the bed. Standing over her, he tossed it at her unceremoniously.

"Put this on and answer me," he ordered. "Do you think I'm the kind of lowlife who doesn't mind where or who he gets off with?"

"You don't have to be so crude about it, but no, I don't think you're that kind of man." She snatched at the towel and gave him a smoldering glare. "If you were, I would never have gotten into this predicament in the first place."

Jesse secured the towel, tucking the ends under over her breasts to keep it in place. Sloan couldn't help but notice that the scanty covering did very little to make her less tempting. He was beginning to think that a burlap sack would be sexy if she wore it. And to even be thinking about it under the circumstances, he felt like even more of a heel. It made him crazy to admit the pull of attraction he still felt for her—even now, when everything in him screamed that it was wrong.

Even if he could never get past all the loyalty and jealousy and pain that bound Michael and Jesse in his thoughts, he knew he would always be drawn to this woman. He hated that he wasn't strong enough to deal with it, and the self-directed hatred made him want to strike back at someone. Jesse, for all her beauty and desirability, was the only target he could get a fix on.

When she tried to smooth things over, Sloan lashed out, fighting with himself to keep from giving in.

"Sloan, can't we forget about this and go on?" She stood and faced him. As they stood eye to eye, Jesse made a convincing case. "I can't help my past. I was Michael's wife. I did love him, but—"

"But what?"

"But time passes. Life doesn't stop."

"Have you been reading greeting cards again, lady?" Sloan rebelled at the clichés she threw at him, even though he had told himself the same things often enough lately. "Next thing I know, you'll be telling me that someday all we'll remember of Michael are the good things, and the pain will be a distant fuzzy memory."

"I'm not saying we won't always hurt when we think about his death, Sloan," she said quietly. "That hurt won't ever go away completely, for either of us. But I don't think Michael would want either of us to spend the rest of our lives crying or running from any happiness we might have because he's gone."

"Yeah, I was waiting for that. What do you know about what Michael would want us to do?" He laughed, and the sound was so harsh it grated on his own ears. "People always seem to get around to justifying whatever they want by saying stuff like that."

"You don't think he would want us to be happy, to go on with our lives?"

"I don't think it's very productive or very healthy of people to spend so much time thinking about what a dead man wants. Or for us to justify our wanting to sleep together by pretending your late husband would give his blessing to it."

He knew he had gone too far as soon as the words left his mouth. Jesse inhaled so sharply that he heard the air hiss through her clenched teeth and come back out as a soft, anguished moan. She reached out with both hands and pushed hard at him, packing enough force in the unexpected action to make him stumble a little.

"You think that's all this is about? Our wanting to sleep together?" Jesse clipped the words out in short, staccato bursts. "If I've misjudged what's going on between us that badly, maybe you should get your clothes and get out of here. Now!"

Sloan moved back another step as she rounded on him. He could see that Jesse was shaking with emotion. It could be rage, hurt, or some combination of the two—he wasn't sure which; but he could tell she was as close to losing her control as he was. Seeing her so upset pulled him out of his own tailspin a bit. He decided that they had both been too caught up by all the emotion of the evening.

He had put her through enough, selfish bastard that he was. It was time to put the brakes on, for now—hell, it was time to get out of her life for good, if this was how it was going to be. Sloan tamped down the tidal wave of disappointment that threatened to swamp him when he realized that he and Jesse were better off without each other.

Get hold of yourself, Lassiter. You aren't going to die over a woman—not even this one. He wasn't sure it was true, but he needed something to keep him from grabbing her and holding on to her for dear life. There would be plenty of time for him to feel sorry for himself later, but right now, all that was important was getting out of the minefield while they both could walk.

"Maybe that's a good idea. But, Jess, I don't want to leave you in this kind of shape." He gentled his voice as much as he could. "We're both keyed up, on edge. I think we should calm down and—"

"Don't you tell me to calm down, Sloan Lassiter!" She tossed her head to shake back the tangle of blond bangs that had fallen over one eye. "This is my house and my life. If I want to scream the walls down, that's just what I'll do. I've spent my whole life being told what to do and how to act, and for a change I'm going to do whatever I feel like. Right now, I don't feel like being calm."

"Come on, Jess. This isn't like you at all."

"Maybe it *is* like me. How would you know?" She held up her hand when he tried to answer. "Excuse me. How could I forget? You know everything about me from Michael, right?"

"Jesse—"

"Oh, no!" she said, slapping one hand briefly over her mouth in an overly dramatic gesture. "We aren't supposed to mention him, are we? Let's keep on putting off using his name or looking at his pictures or admitting either of us ever had anything to do with him. That way, we won't have to face reality at all, will we?"

"That's enough, Jesse."

"Like hell it is!"

"Since when did you start swearing?"

"Since I met you," she snapped. "You'd make a preacher swear, and don't try to change the subject. We were talking about you and me and Michael."

"Yeah, that's all we ever talk about, and that's the problem."

"No, the problem is that we don't talk about it enough to be able to let it go. You clam up or get mad or evade the issue every time anything comes up that involves Michael. Especially since you and I have been getting closer." Her voice wavered, but she swallowed hard and went on. "Tonight was a little more dramatic than usual, but it was all part of the pattern. You want me—"

"Yeah, I'd say that's pretty obvious," he interrupted, raking his hand back through his hair as though he'd just as soon pull it out in frustration. "I'll go so far as to admit what I feel for you goes a lot further than just wanting, too. If that's all it was, there wouldn't be much of a problem. At least, not for long, but—"

"But you can't deal with wanting me or having anything more meaningful between us because Michael's dead and you feel guilty because you're still alive."

"That's a bunch of simple-minded bull."

"Simple-minded, maybe, but it's true anyway." She looked him straight in the eye as she continued. "You want to have me and to be with me, and it's making you act like a crazy man."

"So now I'm crazy?"

"No, of course you're not crazy, Sloan."

"Then don't give me the nickel armchair-psychiatrist bit. I've had enough of that to last me a lifetime."

"I'm sorry. I don't mean to analyze you." Jesse shook her head, causing a few tendrils of hair to float down over her eyes. "But instead of dealing with what you're feeling, you get scared because you keep confusing our being together with all the blame you feel over Michael."

Sloan fought the urge to brush back the lock of hair, telling himself it would be smarter to reach out and shake her. He dismissed the idea, knowing it wouldn't do for him to get that close, even if he pushed away the tenderness. Putting his hands on her at all was courting something too primal. Despite all the runaway emotions of the last couple of hours, she looked rumpled and sexy enough that he was afraid he'd pull her back into his arms. If that happened, there would be no stopping him from claiming her for his own.

"Ah, hell. I don't think we're getting anywhere with this. All we do is go around and around in circles. You act like this is the first crisis I've ever had to deal with." He gave a short, bitter bark of laughter. "I did have a life before I met your husband, complete with a job that specialized in dealing with one crisis after another. What makes you think I can't handle any problems that come up, to be with someone I care for?"

"And you'd like to be with me?" The first hint of a smile he'd seen all evening flirted around the corners of her full lips. "Is that what you're trying to say?"

Deep inside his chest, the hard knot of despair eased a cautious fraction. Sloan tried to squash the tiny ember of optimism before it flared into a flame he couldn't easily put out. *No sense in setting yourself up for a hard fall, Lassiter. Just because she halfway smiles at you doesn't mean anything's changed. Don't let things get out of control again.*

"I didn't say anything of the sort. Even if I wanted to . . ." Sloan knew he was close to making a commitment—closer than he'd ever been before. The thought made him start to sweat. "I'm not the kind of man to make you happy. I'm a hard bastard, not the kind of home-and-hearth, salt-of-the-earth man you need."

"Shouldn't I get a vote in deciding the kind of man I need?"

"I saw at first hand, your kind of man, Jess. Michael was perfect for you. He would have settled down, happily ever after, if it hadn't been for a bad break. I haven't spent two years in a single place for as long as I remember. What kind of risk would I be?"

"I'm not afraid of taking a chance with you, Sloan," she said without hesitation. "What makes you think I want to spend the rest of my life living in a vine-covered cottage? I've been planted in this little corner of the world so long I'm getting root bound. I don't think it would be so terrible to travel around for a while. Especially if it was with you."

"Be careful, talking like that."

"Like what?"

"Insinuating that you'd take off with me. You haven't got much sense of self-preservation, have you?"

"Exactly what do I need to preserve myself from?" Jesse cocked her head to one side and looked at him, half smiling, half seriously. "Are you planning to have your way with me and then sell me into white slavery? You don't look like the type."

"Don't get cute. You have a home here. A home and old friends and a job you like a lot."

"This is my grandparents' vacation home. I can make new friends, and a good teacher can find a job almost anywhere."

"I don't know that I'll find something where I can stay in one place long enough for you to teach for a year. My work has been pretty much all over the place."

"I wouldn't mind traveling for a while, seeing the places you go."

"Some of the places I go aren't safe enough to take a wi—" Sloan stopped short, knowing the next word out of his mouth was going to be *wife*. "A woman," he finished lamely. "You ought to know all about the dangers of my line of work."

Jesse was quiet for a minute, but her eyes sparkled and he knew she had figured out what he had been about to say. *A wife.* His knees literally weakened, hearing the word in his mind, knowing suddenly how much he wanted to think of her in that role. *Good God, Lassiter. A wife. You have to be nuts, man.* When had he stopped thinking of her as a lover and started wanting her for a wife?

"Don't look now, but you're turning a little green around the gills, Sloan." He knew she was teasing him, but there was no doubt that she was pleased by his revelation. The light in her eyes was incandescent. "Are you that afraid of women in general, or is it me in particular?"

"It's you, lady. No doubt about it. You scare me to death."

"Little old me?" She batted her eyelashes, trying to be camp, but the effect was seriously sexy. "I'm harmless."

"So's a handgun, until you pull the trigger."

"I'm not armed." She laughed. "And I'm hardly dressed to be carrying a concealed weapon."

"You're hardly dressed, period."

"My mother always said a good hostess didn't dress up more than her guests." Jesse flushed under his pointed scrutiny, then checked the ends of her towel to make sure they were securely fastened, tugging it upward to cover her breasts more modestly. "You established the dress code tonight, if I'm not mistaken."

He had been trying to keep his mind off the thought of all the delectable skin hidden beneath the bath towel, but she wasn't making things any easier for him. Watching her, thinking about having her for more than a brief and hurried evening, was making him uncomfortably aware of his own state of undress.

"Yeah, I guess I did." He resisted the urge to adjust his own towel, deciding it would be better to go back downstairs and find his clothes. "But I think now would be a good time for me to get dressed and get out of here."

"Okay. That's probably a good idea." Jesse nodded and crossed her arms self-consciously across her chest. The movement only made her look more vulnerable and exposed. "Give me a few minutes and I'll be right down."

"No, that's not necessary." Sloan went to the door and stood there, feeling a little safer for the distance from her and the bed. "Why don't you go on to bed? I'll lock up and let myself out. It's getting pretty late."

"It's not that late," Jesse said, her voice soft and warm. "Let me make you some coffee before you go."

"Maybe next time. I have to leave early tomorrow morning and the caffeine won't let me sleep." He gave her a halfhearted grin. "Not that I'm likely to sleep much anyway, after tonight."

"You're leaving town so soon?" The disappointment was written all over her face. "I thought you were going to be here for a while."

"I thought about it, but right now, I think a couple of days getting my head straight might be a good idea." He tried to sound calm and rational, although the idea of leaving Jesse was tearing him up. "I have an interview with a big company up in Denver in a couple of days—a really good job that will keep me in this part of the country most of the year, if I take it."

"Would you be satisfied settling in one place after all your years of globe-trotting, Sloan? Colorado is beautiful, but it might seem a little boring after all the exciting places you're used to."

"Not all the places I've been in are as glamorous as you imagine, Jess." *Especially after three scenic years in a nine-by-twelve room.* "I like this part of the world. It lets a man breathe."

"And you don't think you'd get itchy feet after a few months?"

He knew she was asking about more than settling for a job. She wanted to know if he was the kind of man who could settle down, and damn it, he didn't know the answer to that, himself. All he was sure about was that if there was a chance that he and Jesse could be together, right now he'd try living on the dark side of the moon without a return ticket home.

"I think it's about time I tried it."

Sloan found he couldn't say more, although he wanted to. He wanted to reassure her that she was the reason he was considering this job. He wished he could say the words to let her know, but there was still too much he had to straighten out in his head. It wouldn't be fair to her—to either of them—for him to mouth easy words before he was certain he could handle everything that was going on between them.

"I'd better go." He edged out into the hall, not wanting to leave, but too smart to stay. The way things stood right now, they both needed time to get their heads back on straight. "I'll call you in a few days. Will that be okay?"

"Better than okay," she whispered. "I'll be waiting."

He turned then and walked away, hearing her call out for him to be careful. Downstairs he glanced at the mess in the kitchen and knew that he should clean it up before he left, but the small voice of reason warned him that if he stayed long enough to do more than dress he might forget everything sensible and head right back upstairs.

"You're a coward, Lassiter," he muttered aloud as he yanked on his shirt and pants and searched for his socks and shoes. "The woman of your dreams is right over your head, and you're running out like a thief in the night."

"Damn straight, old son," he answered as he stuffed his shirttail into his pants and headed for the front door. "All I expected out of this heist was to relieve the lady of a few hours of her time. But this burglary business is more dangerous than it looks. This time the tables got turned and the thief got his heart stolen right out from under him."

Sloan closed the door behind him and stepped out onto the porch. The night air was clean and cool as he drew it into his lungs. Instead of clearing his head, though, it shot into his bloodstream like ninety-proof whiskey, making him drunk with satisfaction. Maybe the air wasn't entirely responsible for the rush of well-being he felt. He grinned and sauntered toward his car.

"No, Lassiter," he mused. "Maybe you have been caught, at last. And just maybe, getting caught might be the best thing that ever happened to you."

13

THE SOUND OF THE FRONT door shutting pulled Jesse out of the dazed state she had been lost in since Sloan walked out of the room. After a moment's reflection, she admitted to herself that she hadn't been quite in control of her emotions concerning the man for a lot longer than this particular night. Since that rainy morning she opened the door to find him glowering at her and dripping all over her floor, her life had changed dramatically.

Changed was a mild word for the difference in her world. She looked down at her body, still wrapped in only a bath towel. She traced a tentative path across her chest and found it still slippery from the cooking-oil massage Sloan had administered. The memory of his hands on her skin made her feel warm all over—warm and shaky and more than a little bit embarrassed by the uninhibited way she had responded to his lovemaking.

Uninhibited. She rather liked the notion that she fit such a gloriously sensual description. No one who had known her in her whole life would ever have used the term *uninhibited* to describe her, she was sure of that. In fact, they would probably be shocked to find that the good Reverend Green's daughter would entertain a man all alone so late at night, much less tremble and sigh in his arms. And those who saw her as the sweet-tempered grade-school teacher would be shocked out of their minds at the thought of her writhing naked and reek-

ing of vegetable oil with a man as worldly and danger-
ous-looking as Sloan Lassiter.

Jesse smiled and settled herself back against the pillows on her bed, replaying her incredible evening. Despite the unfortunate incident with the photograph and
all the talk about Michael, the evening left her with a
sense of hope as well as a healthy dose of good, old-
fashioned fear. How could she be in love with him? It
was so fast, so intense. So new. What she'd had with
Michael hadn't prepared her for this kind of experience. And although she wasn't normally a gambler, at
this moment she would bet anything she owned that
Sloan Lassiter was in love with her just as she was with
him.

He'd never said it in so many words, but it was
there—in his eyes, in the way he kissed and held her.
Since she and Michael had been sweethearts from the
time they were children, she didn't really have much
experience with men—but she knew it all the same.
There was a sureness in her heart, an almost-musical
resonance that rang pure and true whenever Sloan held
her in his arms. She had never heard the music so
clearly before—not even with her husband. Sloan
might not hear bells when they were together, but she
knew that what he felt was more than simple desire.

In the time they had spent talking and getting to
know each other, she had learned to read him pretty
well. He was honest to a fault and blunt enough to make
her cringe at times, but there was no doubting his in-
tegrity. His loyalty to Michael alone would have kept
him from making any move in her direction if he didn't
feel more than a purely sexual urge.

Besides, he had cared enough about her not to make
a big deal of it when he found out she wasn't protected

from getting pregnant. It would have taken very little persuasion for her to have taken a foolish chance with him. She wasn't careless, and an unplanned pregnancy would have been the last thing she wanted to risk, but in the passion of the moment, it would have been all too easy to give in. Sloan not only hadn't gotten upset or made her feel gauche, he'd made love to her with a lack of selfishness that she had never experienced. Someone who was only interested in a casual fling wouldn't have given a damn about her feelings if he was frustrated. Any other man—

Thank goodness, Sloan wasn't any other man. Jesse sat up on the edge of the bed. If she didn't stop all this mooning about, reliving the last few hours and recalling the past few weeks, she would still be sitting here this time tomorrow, wearing only a towel and the silly smile that thinking of Sloan brought to her lips.

There was also the problem that thinking of Sloan made her yearn for all the things they hadn't done with each other—all the talking and touching they couldn't do since he was gone. Fantasizing was fine until compared to reality, then it became self-inflicted torture. She should put those thoughts out of her mind or there was a better-than-average chance she would lose her mind over the next few days.

The clock on the nightstand announced that it was already after midnight. She reluctantly got up and took a shower, finding it took three latherings to get all the traces of oil that had soaked the back length of her hair. In retrospect, she decided it was worth all the shampoo it took for the job. It had been so wonderful to feel a man's touch.

After slipping into a nightshirt, she wrapped her hair turban-style in a towel and brushed her teeth, intending to go directly to bed. Unfortunately, the minty taste of the toothpaste triggered a sudden onset of hunger pangs.

"Forget it," she said, firmly warning her stomach that it could wait until morning. "There's no way you're going to eat again this late."

She unwrapped the towel, brushed the tangles from her damp hair, and switched off the bathroom light. Ignoring the faint, grumbly voice of her appetite, she marched into her room and resolutely turned down the covers on the bed. The grumbles grew into full-fledged growls, demanding to be fed.

"You are not going to go downstairs in the middle of the night and pig out," she informed her insistent stomach. "You have more self-discipline than that."

She got into bed and switched off the light. The comforter was warm and welcoming to her tired body. Deliciously warm. Delicious. *Like hot cocoa and cookies.* No, that wasn't a good word, she thought, trying to weed out such tempting thoughts. Just warm.

She turned over and shifted her head against the fluffy white pillow. *Soft and fluffy as a big marshmallow.* Her subconscious was working overtime, turning traitor along with her stomach. Darn it, you two. Shut up and let me go to sleep!

Closing her eyes tightly, Jesse willed her body to relax. She tried all the old remedies she could think of to turn her mind off food and on to sleep. Counting sheep reminded her of lamb chops. Visualizing a quiet beach scene brought back memories of a clambake. Finally, she decided to let her mind drift, clearing away all thoughts—just letting herself float and dream. Sloan...

Sloan! Not again. This hunger was far stronger than her urge for food—stronger and a lot harder to appease, under the circumstances. She got up and flipped on the light. Cookies and milk didn't sound like such a bad idea, after all. Maybe she could eat herself into satiation. Of course, by the time she did see him again, Sloan might mistake her for the Goodyear blimp.

She padded down to the kitchen barefoot, berating herself for giving in to the call of the cookies. "Temptations of the flesh," her father would have admonished. However, Jesse remembered several times over the years when she had gone to her parents' kitchen to raid the refrigerator and found the good reverend had beaten her to the draw. The smile of remembrance faded from her lips when she walked in and switched on the overhead light.

A sickly frown replaced her smile as she surveyed the mess in the kitchen. Somehow she had forgotten the chaotic aftermath of the frenzied interlude with Sloan. But there it was—the unmistakable evidence of her lack of control. The gnawing hunger that had lured her downstairs vanished, leaving in its place a faint queasiness.

Sloan must have taken his clothes and turned off the light, but everything else was just as they had left it. Her slacks and panties in a crumpled heap on the floor, along with her sneakers and socks. How had Sloan managed to untie her shoes without ever once breaking the spell he had woven around her?

Her shirt had been flung away and had landed under the table. And her bra—she shut her eyes to block out how she had shivered as he had stroked away the lacy item—had somehow ended up hanging half in, half out of the sink. She picked up the bra, cringing with distaste as she noticed one strap had fallen into a dinner plate she had left there. A strand of half-dried pasta came up with the strap. She removed it and tossed it back onto the plate, wrinkling her nose.

She began to pick up the other scattered clothing, trying not to imagine how tawdry the scene must have looked to Sloan when he came down to dress. The place was in a shambles, looking nothing at all like the neat and orderly room it usually was. Removing the discarded clothes and taking them into the laundry room gave her some hope of regaining control. She started the washing machine and went back to tackle the dishes.

It didn't take long for her to scrape and rinse the plates and stack them in the dishwasher. The more onerous task of washing down the oily cabinets and mopping the floor took quite a while, but the hot, sudsy water, smelling of lemon, freshened the air and gave her a sense of regaining her composure. She focused on the cleaning, ruthlessly diverting her mind to another train of thought any time images of her and Sloan together crept in. By the time she had the house back to normal, it was closer to dawn than midnight.

She knew she would be tired all day, but there was no way she could go back to sleep after everything that had happened. Her mind was still turning over the events of the day and sifting back through the months that had led her to this point. How could she have remained so contentedly celibate, and then fallen so hard and fast for a virtual stranger? *Okay,* she admitted as her conscience nudged her, *maybe not content, exactly. But I was celibate.*

She sighed and put on a pot of coffee. Maybe it would help to go outside before the sun was up and take her daily run early. Then she could work in the yard for a while.

She quickly changed into a comfortable sweat suit and running shoes, and pulled her hair back into a loose ponytail. Instead of putting on any makeup, she just avoided looking in the mirror. Since Sloan was gone, there wouldn't be anyone around to see her, so if she wanted to have one day to be sloppy, where was the harm?

The moon was full and still bright enough for her to be able to see as she ran. Jesse breathed in the crisp air, grateful that she lived in a place where a woman running alone was safe. There was very little chance of meeting anything more dangerous than a raccoon or one of the Wilsons' big, friendly dogs. She set a comfortable pace and turned her attention to her breathing and stride, purposefully trying to clear her head of all her problems. It worked surprisingly well for a couple of miles.

Then, as she began her return lap, all at once Jesse found herself unable to run any farther. She felt as if she had been hit by an invisible force that drained all her strength and energy in a single, voracious gulp. One minute she was racing up the gentle hill just behind her property; the next, it was all she could do to reach the top of the slight rise before she stumbled to a halt.

Her legs quite literally refused to move. Her breath came in ragged gasps as she struggled to take in enough air to keep from passing out. Her head buzzed and for a moment the night darkened as she almost passed out. She sank to the ground, glad that it was soft and grassy rather than covered with rock or cactus.

"Head between your knees," she ordered, remembering all the years she had heard other people given that sage advise. "Get your head down and stay calm."

So she sat cross-legged on the ground and hugged her knees, waiting for the dizziness to pass. She was more surprised than frightened by the situation—her health was excellent, she had no history of anything that might have caused this to happen. And gradually, the world around her settled back to normal, including her ability to concentrate and breathe regularly. It had to be exhaustion. That and a lack of anything much to eat for the whole day and night. She had been so busy getting ready for Sloan's return that she hadn't eaten until dinnertime last night, and then so much had happened that she'd barely tasted the meal they had together.

Yes, that was all that was wrong. Jesse cautiously lifted her head and took her bearings. Good. She wasn't far from the house. The back porch lights shone reassuringly only several hundred feet away.

The little hill she sat on was the old Indian burial mound, she realized with relief. As she tried to stand, her legs trembled and she decided to sit and rest for a bit longer before she went on to the house. She lay back against the cushion of grass and folded her arms behind her head—might as well be as comfortable as possible until her strength returned.

Jesse looked up at the canopy of stars above her, marveling for the hundredth time at the brightness and vastness of the New Mexico sky. Out here there were no city lights to dim their intensity or obscure the glittering beauty of their patterns. She sought out the Big and Little Dippers. And there was Orion, standing eternal vigil over the night. She liked the peace in spite of her predicament and gave way to the lassitude that enveloped her. The last thing she noticed before her eyes closed was the double ring that encircled the full moon.

She might have stayed there until morning except for the mournful hooting of a night owl. The sound repeated and echoed in her ears, drawing her out of her sleep. At least she *thought* she was awake. When she opened her eyes, things around her were so different, Jesse was disoriented for a few seconds. She could still see the porch light in the distance, but it was diffused and blurred by ragged wisps of fog that had come from nowhere.

Jesse sat up and rubbed at her eyes as if the action would clear her vision. It was no use. The fog was real, obscuring the stars and moon except for an occasional glimpse as the low-lying clouds drifted past on their way to the mountains. The old burial ground looked different now. Wreathed in curls of mist and vapor, it seemed truly a place of mystery and wonder—an ancient place where ghosts of dead warriors would surely be welcome.

There was a faint rustle just behind her and Jesse looked around to see its source. Nothing. Then to her right came a soft scraping that might have been footsteps. She turned and peered into the shadows.

"Who's there?"

No answer. Only the quietness of the night. Jesse laughed aloud, nervous in spite of her knowledge that there was nothing there except in her mind. She stood and stretched, ready to get back to the light and warmth of her house.

After one hesitant step she was stopped dead in her tracks, hearing again a barely audible noise. She couldn't quite figure out where the sound was coming from—her sense of direction was muddled by the enveloping fog.

"Silver Wolf?"

She knew it was silly, but she felt a presence, a *something* out there. Maybe it was the old Indian Michael had sworn walked in this place.

"Silver Wolf. Is it you?" Again there was a sound, as if in answer to her question. Jesse was amazed to find herself unafraid—more than unafraid, even eager to see the old ghost. "Is anybody there?"

"Michael . . ."

The thought came to her suddenly, raising the hair on the back of her neck. It wouldn't be surprising to find him here in this place he loved so much.

"Michael?"

She stood very still and looked around, waiting and watching for some sign. Minutes passed, but there was no reply, no sound but her own breathing. Not a trace of him remained—except in her heart. He was gone. Forever.

She waited for the terrible wave of loss to come flooding over her, but instead there was only a bittersweet nostalgia. As she stood there, saying her own silent goodbye, the first rays of the sun came over the horizon and diffused the mist, sending the low clouds back into the sky.

Jesse turned and walked slowly down the path to the house. Her steps were halting and a little unsteady at first. Resisting the temptation to turn and look back over her shoulder, she finally accepted that the past was truly behind her.

She had to live now, in this time. And she wanted to spend the rest of the time she had with the man she loved. Now, all that mattered was convincing Sloan that their time was about to begin.

"IT'S ABOUT TIME!"

Sloan looked down at his watch for the third time in fifteen seconds as he waited for the elevator to make its way from the second to the first floor. He was going to be late, and the elevators in this place were brass-trimmed, mirror-lined snails.

"Why do all the big shots have to have their offices above the twentieth floor?" he grumbled. "It would save a lot of time if they took over the lower floors and let all the peasants waste their time riding up and down in this old clunker."

He didn't expect an answer. The only other person in the elevator car was a gray-haired lady in a power suit who had been avoiding eye contact with him, obviously not wanting to get involved in the slightest degree with a hard-faced man who talked to himself in public places.

You're going to have to watch it, Lassiter. He switched to a silent mode. *If you really plan to work in the concrete jungle, you're going to have to learn to play by the rules. Rule number one: People are going to think you're loony tunes if you don't stop carrying on conversations with both sides of your head.*

"That's more like it!"

He broke rule number one as the elevator bottomed out and the door slid slowly open. Stepping aside to let the woman go ahead of him, he looked out into the lobby of the corporate headquarters of the Merlin Corporation. It was a place of soaring high ceilings and suitably high-tech decor, a fitting home for the central offices of one of the fastest-growing computer companies in the country—his new place of employment as of five minutes ago.

When Sloan had walked in for his interview with personnel, he'd been surprised to be shown right in to the head of the corporation. It had been even more of a shock to find that the chief executive officer of the multimillion-dollar business was a skinny guy half his own age. Samuel "Merlin" Jones could have been mistaken for a college student, dressed as he was in jeans and a sweatshirt.

Sloan had felt as old as Methuselah and stiffly overdressed in his conservative gray suit. Old—and sure that he was not at all the kind of person they would want in a place like this. But it hadn't taken long for him to change his mind. Merlin had put him at ease by giving him a tour of the offices and introducing him to the staff. In a few minutes, Sloan had realized the youthful exterior hid the kind of brains and drive that it had to have taken to build this megamonster enterprise.

He'd liked Merlin's enthusiasm and admired the innovative and aggressive nature of the company, but he still wasn't sure where he was needed. Merlin had filled him in, painting an industry where time and efficiency were as valuable as innovative ideas. He'd informed Sloan that they had to have a man of action who could keep an eye on the competition and pinpoint potential internal bottlenecks. They needed someone who had a working knowledge of international business and who could make decisions in a hurry, if necessary. Most of the problems could be handled from Denver, but there would be occasional trips to Japan and Europe.

Merlin had assured Sloan that his limited knowledge of computers wasn't a problem. They had more than enough people who handled the product end of things, he'd said wryly, and plenty of bean counters. What they were lacking was a middleman, a troubleshooter who could deal with snafus and give the company some corporate muscle. Sloan had found himself agreeing to take the position, and they'd sealed things with a handshake.

So here he was, standing out in the warm Denver sunshine, having just landed a plum job with a hot company, walking free after three years of confining hell—and none of it would mean a damn thing if the next couple of hours didn't turn out okay. As he headed for the parking lot to get his car, his stomach knotted with a mixture of dread and anticipation.

Jesse. It all came down to Jesse.

He couldn't get the woman off his mind. On the long drive from Taos to Denver, the only thing he'd been able to think of was Jesse. He had replayed every conversation they'd ever had, recalled every time they'd been together. No matter how he stacked the deck, no matter which way he tried to find another answer, his only conclusion was that he was totally and undeniably in love with Jesse Varner. And it didn't feel as if he had any hope of getting over it.

Hell, the scary thing was that he *didn't want* to get over it.

As soon as he checked in at his hotel and got to his room, he'd found himself picking up the phone and dialing her number. She was surprised to hear from him so soon, but she had sounded glad, all the same. Glad, but very strained. After talking for a couple of minutes about almost nothing, he'd ended the conversation and left her his number, just in case she needed something.

When she'd called him back later in the evening, his first thought was that there was an emergency. She had denied anything was wrong, but in the next breath, she'd told him she had to see him. It couldn't wait until he got through with his trip. She was coming to Denver.

The news had raised goose bumps on the back of his neck. Something was wrong. He'd heard the tension in her voice, and the fact that she was coming all the way to Denver to talk didn't sound so good. He'd tried to get her to tell him what was on her mind, but she'd been evasive, saying only that it was vital and that she would be arriving the following day. He'd agreed to meet her at her hotel this afternoon, and he was a man of his word.

What in the world could she want? He had no way of knowing whether she was coming to tell him she wanted to be with him, or if she had given in to second thoughts and was ready to kiss him off. Surely she wasn't stupid enough to break the news in person. Either possibility was equally frightening.

He wanted her so much it was making him crazy. In his whole life there had never been a woman that he had considered settling down with, raising a family with. Oh, there had been a couple of times he'd been involved enough to be exclusive for a few months, but even from the beginning of those relationships he had never had this kind of knowing—this certainty that "always" wouldn't be half long enough.

He was in love for real, and he wanted it all this time. That was certain as far as he was concerned, but he was far from being sure that he was the right man for Jesse. She deserved someone kinder, someone gentler—the kind of man she'd had the first time.

"Don't get started on that track again, Lassiter," he admonished. "You'll drive yourself really crazy if you aren't careful." He looked at himself in the rearview mirror and shook his head. "That is, if you haven't already crossed the line. Just hang on until you talk to her. Then we'll see if it's time to call the guys in the white coats."

THE FLOWERS WERE arranged. The sitting area was cozy. There was a bottle of white wine chilling in the ice bucket. Jesse looked critically around the hotel suite.

All that was missing was Sloan.

Another glance convinced her the room was as ready as it was ever going to be. She wished she could say the same for herself. Her nerves were tied in knots, anticipation warring with dread. All she could do was pace the confines of the small suite and bide her time. He should have been here by now.

For want of anything else to do except think, Jesse went into the bathroom and freshened her lipstick. Her face was pale—a sure sign of tension—so she stroked on a little more blush. A definite improvement. She had left her hair down, fluffed into a mass of full waves that fell past her shoulders. It was a blatantly sexy style, but perfect with her simple dress and pumps.

Jesse smiled at herself in the mirror as she straightened the V neckline of her belted shift. On the hanger the dress was unremarkable, but she knew just how deceiving simplicity could be. The rich teal color made her tan look even deeper, and there was nothing on earth like the luster and flow of real silk. It felt good against her body and gave her a sense of confidence. And she hadn't picked out her most flattering heels just because they went with the dress, either.

Every single thing she had on, from the shoes to the gold hoops in her ears, was chosen to make her look and feel her very best. She had bathed and misted herself all over with her favorite perfume, blushing a bit at some of the places she concentrated the fragrance. She didn't bother to kid herself about her intentions. There was only one reason for her being here, for her primping and pacing. She wanted to make a good impression on Sloan Lassiter. More than a good impression, to be perfectly honest. She wanted to knock him off his feet.

It might be easy for some women to play seduction games, but she was more of a novice at this sort of thing than a lot of sixteen-year-old girls. It crossed her mind that she might be being *too* obvious. Maybe the dress and the sexy hair and the high heels were overkill. Maybe the flowers were too much. Maybe—

Her last-minute worries were cut short by the sound of a knock on the door. A very familiar knock.

Her stomach tightened. He was here! There was no more time for second-guessing or rearranging. The rest of her life depended on what happened right now.

Jesse muttered a quick but fervent prayer under her breath as she walked the few steps to the door. When she opened it and took a look at Sloan's face, she wished she had devoted more than a couple of seconds to praying. Divine intervention might come in handy, if the stony expression on his face was any indicator of his mood.

Lord! If ever there was a hard-looking man, he was standing right in front of her. There wasn't a trace of a smile, not even a slight social quirk of his lips. In fact, he was so serious that she thought his face might literally crack if he were to try smiling. Nor was she encouraged by the narrowed focus of his eyes, so cold and dark that the blue was as steely and unyielding as gunmetal.

"Sloan."

He merely looked at her and nodded. She resisted the urge to turn tail and run, and even managed to hold on to her nerve enough to continue.

"You're here," she said, cringing at the inane greeting. "Come in."

She was nervous, and he didn't make it any easier when he stepped inside without a word and stood waiting for her to make the next move. Ignoring the urge to make small talk to defuse the awkwardness of the situation, she gathered up her courage and stood her ground, returning his silent stare.

He looked wonderful, despite all the glowering. Dressed in a dark business suit, he looked every inch the cool industrial power-hitter. His mere physical presence was enough to intimidate—let alone the backing of the cartels he was used to representing. No wonder he was in such demand when corporate arm-twisting was needed.

But this was private life, not business, and she doubted he was quite as cool and controlled as he appeared outwardly. She doubted that he would have gotten involved with her in the first place if he'd had any choice in the matter. Yet, even if he was intent on maintaining this air of cold disinterest, she knew it was only an act. After all, he was here and that had to count for something. Jesse screwed up her courage and broke the deadlock of silence.

"Let's not stand here glaring at each other, okay?" He didn't thaw, so she tried again. "Don't you think you'd be more comfortable sitting? That way you can glare at me while I get you something to drink."

He had the grace to mumble something that might have been an apology and allowed himself to be led to a couch. Although he sat down, she could tell he was anything but relaxed. His posture was defensive—sitting a bit too far forward, as if he wanted to be able to get up quickly, should the need arise—not the look of a man about to let down his guard.

He didn't say anything, but she noticed him checking out the room, noting the wine, lifting his eyebrows a fraction when he saw the flowers. As she poured the wine, he seemed to relax a little, at least enough to settle back against the cushion. Jesse was relieved when he took the glass from her fingers and looked up at her, his gaze not quite so flinty. Maybe he had decided to give her a chance.

She breathed a little easier. This was going to be hard enough without having to fight him every step of the way. She didn't know exactly how to begin, although she had planned and mentally rehearsed her speech a dozen times over the last couple of days. In her daydreams, things had been much easier, not like this, with him sitting and staring up at her, making her feel like a Broadway actress standing center stage who had suddenly forgotten her lines.

She wiped her damp palms down the sides of her skirt under the pretense of smoothing invisible wrinkles from the fabric. Lord help her, she couldn't just blurt everything out—not without making a total fool of herself. What if he wasn't as serious as she believed? What if he didn't really want to be involved? What if—

"Aren't you going to have anything to drink?" Sloan took a healthy swallow and nodded appreciatively. "This is pretty good stuff."

"Not right now, thank you." She was glad he'd said something. Even making polite social chitchat was better than just standing here like an idiot. "I don't drink much."

"That's not how I remember it." There was a smile hidden in his words.

"You don't have to bring that up." She stopped the automatic explanation of her old indiscretion. "Let's just agree that I don't handle liquor too well sometimes. Right now I need to keep a clear head."

"Why now?" he asked, making her even more nervous as he watched her closely. "If this is so important, shouldn't I keep my head clear, too? Or are you trying to get me drunk, so you can take advantage of me?"

"Of course I'm not trying to get you drunk," she said indignantly. "And I certainly don't want to take advantage of you."

"That's a pity."

"What is that supposed to mean?"

"Nothing, Jess." He finished the wine in a couple of long gulps and put the glass down on the table. "And before you ask: No, I don't want another drink. Or a cigarette. Or anything else you have to offer. Just tell me whatever it is you got me over here for."

"I'm getting to that," she said, smoothing her skirt again. "But I don't know exactly where to start and . . . and it's making me nervous."

"It's making *you* nervous?" Sloan sounded incredulous. "What in the hell do you think you're doing to *my* nerves?"

"You? You're scared, too?"

"That's putting it mildly." Sloan shifted on the sofa and tugged on his tie, loosening it and turning the knot a fraction askew. "I've been in more than my share of tough situations, but I don't think I've ever been any more worried."

"Really?" She touched the narrow gold chain around her neck and absently straightened the collar of her dress, not able to keep her hands still. "You must be a heck of a poker player, then."

"Poker's only a game, Jess. I have a feeling neither of us is here to play games today."

Jesse stopped fidgeting and took a moment to study him. He did seem to be ill at ease, come to think of it. Not that it was easy to tell, with that hard stoicism he wore like a suit of armor. But there were telltale signs that he was uncomfortable—an occasional twitch of a nerve in his jaw, the way he raked one hand back through his hair, leaving it a bit untidy.

No, he wasn't totally in control, either. Somehow, the knowledge made her less terrified to talk to him. Jesse gathered up her courage and sat on the couch beside him, careful to leave a safe distance between them.

"You're right, Sloan. I didn't ask you here to play games. I have something very serious to talk to you about, but..."

He didn't say a word to make things easier, but she knew she had his undivided attention. He was watching her intently, and there was a shadow of something she couldn't quite read in his eyes.

"Okay, Sloan. I needed to talk to you about..."

She stopped once again and broke eye contact with him. It was too hard to look at him so directly—eyes gave everything away. How could she stand seeing rejection reflected there? She laced her fingers together and looked down at them clenched in her lap.

"This is hard and I don't know the right way to tell you—"

"Hell's bells, Jesse!" His voice wasn't loud, but it had a raw edge of passion. "Don't keep me hanging. Just tell me. If you don't want me to come around anymore, for God's sake, just tell me straight."

"What?" Her head jerked up and she looked at him as if he were crazy. "What are you talking about?"

"Is that what's so hard for you to tell me? That you've had time to think about it and you don't want me coming around anymore?" His voice was hoarse and there was no longer any attempt to hide his agitation. "I know why you had me meet you here. Denver's a long way from your cozy little house in Taos, isn't it, Jess?"

"You think I came all this way just to keep you away from my house?"

Jesse could hardly believe the wild tangent his imagination had taken. She had made such big plans and broken all land-speed records to get here to see him, and the man thought it was a brush-off. All that kept her from screaming in frustration was the fact that he was obviously upset by the notion. It wasn't rejection she saw in the depths of his blue eyes, but fear that *she* didn't want *him*.

The man was crazy—as crazy as she was. Crazy with love. Nothing else would account for the strained expression and general paranoia. She had experienced the same anguish and uncertainty of loving and not being loved in return. She couldn't mistake the symptoms. Sympathy for his condition was matched by relief that he was as deeply afflicted as she was.

"Don't jump to conclusions, Sloan. You aren't very good at deductive reasoning." She found herself able to talk now, released from the fear that he didn't care for her. "If I didn't want to see you anymore, don't you think a phone call would have been a lot simpler?"

"Nothing between us has ever been simple. Why should I expect it to start now?"

"It can start now, Sloan. We can stop throwing up barriers and make it the simplest thing in the world." Jesse looked directly at him, willing him to believe. "But one of us has to be the first to take a chance—to say the words that make everything else unimportant. That's why I asked you here. I want to tell you that I love you."

If she hoped for an immediate and mutual declaration, she would have been devastated. She knew him too well for that. Instead, she waited, watching him deal with her blunt statement. He was a guarded man, not used to openly discussing his private feelings, and she expected it to take a minute to sink in, but Sloan was silent for so long that Jesse was ready to scream. If she hadn't seen the response in his face before he hid it, she might have believed she was wrong. But no matter what other problems they had, that one hot flicker of love had flamed so true that there was no way she was mistaken.

"I love you, Sloan." The words were barely a whisper this time, and she held out her left hand to him. "I've put the past behind me and come to you in hopes that you can do the same."

"I'm real damn tired of the past, honey," he said. "There's nothing I'd rather do than let it go."

Sloan took her hand and looked at it, noticing the difference immediately. He gently traced the white line on her third finger, caressing the pale band of skin against her tan—the only visible remainder of her marriage to Michael.

"When did you take it off?"

"The night you left." Jesse closed his fingers around and was rewarded by the hard pressure of his hand enfolding hers. "I knew before then that I loved you, but it took you to make me make the final break—to finally be able to put things away that belong to another time."

"It takes more than removing a ring to do that, Jess." Sloan shook his head, but his grip on her hand tightened almost to the point of causing pain. "Are you sure you aren't holding on to me because I'm your last link to Michael? I don't think I could live with that."

"I've said my goodbyes to Michael." Jesse didn't try to loosen his grip. She didn't care how tightly he held on—it could never be enough for her. He didn't want to let go of her; that was the most important thing. "I should be the one asking if you're over all your doubts about being with me."

"I don't have any doubts about how I feel about you."

"Are you sure you aren't still feeling guilty for wanting Michael's wife?"

"You aren't Michael's wife anymore." There was no hesitation in his answer. "I rode that horse a long time, but it finally died, thank God. If Michael walked through that door right now—alive and well—you'd still be mine. I'd fight for you and use anything it took, fair or foul. I'd fight and I'd win. I'd win because you aren't his now. You're a different woman from the Jesse Michael loved—and a damn sight different woman from the one who loved him."

"I *am* different, Sloan." Jesse pressed on, wanting more. "I've always been a different person than the woman you came to see."

"And I came because of a promise and a fantasy. It had nothing to do with you. All the guilt I felt was over a dream—an imaginary woman who looked a lot like you." He smiled then—a real smile that touched her to her soul. "You aren't something I have to be ashamed of loving, Jess. You're real. If there hadn't been something between us, the dream would have faded and I would have walked away. I don't love you because you were Michael's wife. I don't even love you in spite of it. I just love you."

"That's all I needed to hear."

Sloan tightened his grip on her hand and pulled her across the distance separating them. The determination in his eyes sparked an answering fire in her belly, set her quivering with anticipation.

"You aren't Michael's wife anymore, sweetness," he whispered. His mouth was a breath away from hers as he lifted her onto his lap. "You've been mine for a long time now."

In some dim corner of her conscious mind, Jesse wanted to answer him, but he never gave her a chance to speak. His mouth covered hers, muting the incoherent sound she made and transforming it into a whimper of need. It was a kiss like none they'd ever shared, like none that ever existed before.

With the fluency of his lips Sloan spoke of his love in ways no words could ever match. All the languages of the world had less power to persuade than the silken touch of his tongue against hers. Jesse gave herself to the poetry of his mouth, letting him tell her every thought in his heart, opening herself to his message without reservation, inviting him to breach the last wall that stood between them.

Sloan didn't hesitate to accept her capitulation. With a groan of need and triumph, he pulled her closer against him, turning her in his arms and lifting her to sit astride him. Her legs parted and she settled down on top of him, bracing her knees against the couch behind them. Their bodies joined as tightly as their mouths, pressing together as closely as the barrier of their clothing allowed—heat against heat, hardness against answering softness.

Jesse encircled him with her arms, kneading the back of his neck with greedy fingers as his mouth continued its ravishing magic. Her fingers slid into his hair, clenching the dark strands as if holding on to a lifeline. Everything in the world was centered on this moment. She thought she would never need anything else. Then Sloan's hands slipped under her skirt to caress the silk-covered backs of her legs, and Jesse realized she needed more than kisses—a lot more.

Sloan broke the kiss then, and pulled his head back just far enough to watch her face. Jesse saw her own longing reflected in his eyes.

"I'm going to have you," he said, pulling her down harder on his body, lifting his hips to punctuate the promise. "I'm going to be inside you, in your body, in your mind. I'm going to be so much a part of you that you'll never be the same again."

His hands cupped her bottom, gripping her with hard fingers that almost—just almost—crossed the line between pleasure and pain. Jesse gasped as he rocked her hips backward and forward, slowly and deliberately rubbing her against his body.

"You feel how much I want you, darling?" he asked. "Can you imagine how good it's going to be when we don't have anything between us?"

He hooked his fingers inside the waistband of her panty hose and peeled them down in a single moment. Jesse lifted her hips to help him without breaking eye contact. Her skin tingled as he massaged the newly bared skin.

A fine sheen of perspiration beaded his upper lip, despite the coolness of the air-conditioned room. She leaned toward him and licked it off like a kitten lapping cream. Sloan's fingers tightened on her rounded bottom and he moaned like a man in pain.

"Stop it, Jesse," he pleaded. "Stop that right now, or I'll never make it long enough to get you to the bed."

She knew he was telling the truth. Without hesitation her tongue came out again, sliding over his upper lip, then darting in and out of the warmth of his mouth.

"I warned you," he growled against her lips. "Baby, I warned you."

Before her next heartbeat she was on her back on the couch with the welcome weight of his body covering her. Sloan made good his promise, urged on by her helping hands. As they kissed and nibbled at each other, impatient fingers fumbled with buttons and belts. Panty hose and tie dropped where they were flung as shoes and socks fell with abandon.

There was only a moment of delay before the storm hit full force. Jesse looked up at Sloan poised above her, the embodiment of the dark stranger of her dreams— better than any dream. This was a real man, a lover whose flesh was as heated as hers, a lover who made her dreams a pale memory.

"This is forever, Jesse." Sloan's eyes burned into her with the clear blue flame of love. "Can you handle that?"

"I can handle anything you want to give me." Jesse wrapped her legs around his waist and pulled him down onto her, shuddering as he thrust inside her. She lifted her arms to encircle his neck and pulled his head to her mouth. They began to move together, and she gave herself totally to the gathering swell of pleasure. "Give me forever, Sloan."

"Forever, sweetness," he promised as the skies fell. "Forever..."

Epilogue

"SLOAN, WAKE UP."

The voice was a whisper in the silence of the night.

"Go away. I'm sleeping."

"Please, Sloan. I need you."

"Shut up!"

He shut his eyes hard, not wanting to see the figure that materialized out of a moonbeam—a woman with hair the color of sunshine on ripe wheat and thick-lashed, heavy-lidded brown eyes that promised all kinds of things.

"I don't see you. I don't want to see you. You aren't real."

"I am real, Sloan," she said insistently. "You can shut your eyes or put your pillow over your head like last night, but I'm still here. Feel me."

And then, as in a hundred dreams of a hundred nights, she was in his arms. He could feel her. Her skin was like honey against his tongue, her arms and legs a velvet trap he never wanted to escape from. Even as he held her and made her his, a tiny part of him knew this was a dream. He fought waking, shivering with the fear that she would disappear and he would be left alone once more in this godforsaken nightmare.

He fought leaving the land of sleep; and the harder he fought, the closer he came to waking. The woman in his arms melted against him like snow against his hot skin, disappearing more rapidly the closer he held her.

"No!" he begged. "Don't go, Jesse. I love you."

J. Sloan Lassiter jerked upright in bed, throwing back the sheet and blanket in a violent motion. He swung his feet to the side of the plain narrow bed and winced as they came in contact with the coldness of the bare floor tiles. He sat for a moment, feeling the slick of sweat from the dream chilling his skin as the night air licked it from his hard-muscled body.

Not a sound broke the stillness. He imagined he could hear the echo of his own voice sinking into the thick walls of his cell. He looked around in the darkness. The faint light of the moon shining through the grillwork over the window enabled him to see his surroundings—a cheap wooden table stacked with books and papers, and a couple of rickety chairs; an old metal footlocker at the end of his bed.

He didn't want to look at the other side of the room. He knew only too well what was there. Michael's bed. The nightmare blended with the room and the room became the nightmare, twisting and turning in his head until he didn't know anymore when he was sleeping and when he was awake.

The dreams lately had seemed so real—more real than usual. Dreams of getting out of this place, of driving a fast sports car across the open plains, of finding Jesse.

This last one had been so real it had seemed to last for months. Jesse as his wife, wearing a big diamond ring and carrying his child. Jesse loving him.

He cursed the darkness, wishing he could stay in the dream instead of this damned murky hell. Then, out of the corner of his eye, he became aware of a glowing brightness. Wrong direction for the guard's flashlight. Wrong time for the sunrise. To his left, in the direction of Michael's bed.

As he turned toward it, the light burst into a glaring white, so bright that he covered his eyes with his hand, momentarily blinded by the strange brilliance. Then the light dimmed to a bearable level, but before he could see again, a voice called his name.

"Sloan. Sloan, old buddy. Wake up."

"Michael?" It couldn't be. Michael was dead. "Michael, is it you? How—"

"Wake up, Sloan. Time for the dreams to stop."

"I *am* awake."

"No, you're not, my friend."

Sloan lowered his hand and looked over into the glowing whiteness. The light had a unique quality—misty as sunshine through raindrops, full of such vitality it almost had a life of its own. And in the center of the radiance was the plain old bed, rendered beautiful by its surroundings. And sitting on the edge of the bed—dressed in white, his hair blown by the force of an unseen gale—was Michael.

Sloan knew this was another of the strange nightly visions, but this one was different. Instead of the fear and loathing of the nightmare, or the heated passion of being with Jesse, this dream was as clean and peaceful as the light that surrounded it. Even the emotions triggered by seeing Michael again were softened and lifted by the glow.

"Michael, this isn't real, is it?" Sloan marveled at the aura of health and well-being apparent on his friend's face. "Man, you look great. But how . . . ?"

"How isn't important, Sloan. Just that I finally got through to you." Michael smiled and his eyes were sparkling like sapphires. "I can't stay long, but you don't need for me to stay anymore, do you, pal?"

"I don't want you to go, Michael. God, but it's great to see you like this. Well and happy." Sloan looked back into the darkness, seeing the grimness of the room in contrast to the purity that enfolded Michael. "Why did you come back to this . . . this place?"

"I came for you, Sloan."

"You came to break me out of here? How are you going to do that?"

"I came so you can break yourself out of here, my friend. All you have to do is let go. Let go of the dreams. Let go of me. Say goodbye to all of this stuff and get on with your life."

"Which life, Michael?" Sloan raked his hand back through his hair and shook his head, trying to focus his mind. "It all gets so tangled, sometimes I don't know what's real and what isn't."

"Only in your dreams." Michael laughed and the sound was filled with music. "You know what's real. Jesse's real. Your love for her is all that should matter anymore. Say goodbye now, Sloan, and go home. Don't come back here again. There's nothing here for you. I'm not here any more than you are. Go home."

"So it's that simple in your mind, Michael? Just go home?"

"It is that easy, pal. Tell me goodbye and get out of here."

Without another word Michael was gone. The light around him brightened like a star gone nova, forcing Sloan to shield his eyes from its increasing brilliance. At the same time, he felt his heart grow lighter, and for the first night in as long as he could remember, the pain was gone.

"Goodbye, Michael."

He lay back on his bed, his arm still over his eyes, and slept. It might have been minutes or hours before he awakened, but the first thing he noticed was the glare of daylight in his face. He turned on his side and peered out through half-closed eyes. What he saw brought a smile to the hard line of his lips.

Jesse. Jesse Lassiter, sleeping in a tangle of long blond hair, her mouth curved in a satisfied smile, her hand resting on her gently rounded breasts. And on the third finger of her hand, the diamonds in her rings scattered the rays of the morning sun like a shower of jewels.

His wife. He looked around the room, identifying their furniture, their paintings on the wall. His house. He reached over and put his hand on the slightly rounded mound of her stomach. His life.

Jesse murmured in her sleep and wriggled closer. He put his arm around her and pulled her to him, snuggling and resting his chin against her tousled hair. This was the best dream of all, he decided. Life—the only dream he needed from now on.

"Goodbye, Michael," he whispered.

He closed his eyes and drifted off into a dreamless sleep.

HARLEQUIN®

my Valentine

1993

The most romantic day of the year is here! Escape into the exquisite world of love with MY VALENTINE 1993. What better way to celebrate Valentine's Day than with this very romantic, sensuous collection of four original short stories, written by some of Harlequin's most popular authors.

**ANNE STUART
JUDITH ARNOLD
ANNE McALLISTER
LINDA RANDALL WISDOM**

**THIS VALENTINE'S DAY, DISCOVER ROMANCE
WITH MY VALENTINE 1993**

Available in February wherever Harlequin Books are sold.   VAL93